"This Is A Bad Idea."

"Probably," Nick agreed, easing to meet Zoë halfway. He caressed her cheek with the tips of his fingers, combed them gently through her hair.

"We agreed this wouldn't happen again."

"Did we? We're already here—the damage has been done. Is one more time really going to make that much of a difference?"

It was hard to argue with logic like that, especially when he was nibbling at her ear. What difference could one more time possibly make? "What goes on in this room stays in this room," Zoë said.

His lips brushed her shoulder and her knees went weak. "Agreed."

Then he kissed her and she melted.

One more time, she promised herself. One more time and they would forget this ever happened....

Dear Reader,

I've found very few things in life as rewarding as rescuing animals. Presently we have three dogs and three cats, ranging in age from six months to ten years old. As I write this letter I have one dog beside me on the couch, one to my left on the floor and yet another on his bed across the room. Two of the cats are in the dining room playing tag and the third is lounging on the back of the couch behind my head.

They are my pals. They love me unconditionally and keep me company while I work. They guard my house and protect my children. Not to mention keep us mouse free. They are a part of the family.

For several years I had toyed with the idea of adopting a retired racing greyhound. I love big dogs, so the size really appealed to me. Last summer I took the plunge and filled out an application on the Web site of our local organization, Regap of Michigan (Retired Greyhounds as Pets). Several weeks later we adopted our first grey. I was so impressed with the organization that when a call went out for volunteers, I was one of the first in line. Words cannot express how rewarding the experience has been. It seemed only natural to pay tribute to these amazing animals through my writing.

Tucker, Nick's greyhound in this book, is based loosely on my own dog, Combat. To learn more about greyhounds check out the Regap site, www.rescuedgreyhound.org.

Best,

Michelle Celmer

THE SECRETARY'S SECRET

MICHELLE CELMER

Published by Silhouette Books
America's Publisher of Contemporary Romance

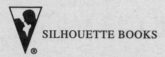

SILHOUETTE BOOKS

ISBN-13: 978-0-373-76774-8
ISBN-10   0-373-76774-9

THE SECRETARY'S SECRET

Copyright © 2007 by Michelle Celmer

This edition published by arrangement with Harlequin Books S.A.

® and TM are trademarks of Harlequin Books S.A., used under license.
Trademarks indicated with ® are registered in the United States Patent
and Trademark Office, the Canadian Trade Marks Office and in other
countries.

Visit Silhouette Books at www.eHarlequin.com

Printed in U.S.A.

Books by Michelle Celmer

Silhouette Desire

Playing by the Baby Rules #1566
The Seduction Request #1626
Bedroom Secrets #1656
Round-the-Clock Temptation #1683
House Calls #1703
The Millionaire's Pregnant Mistress #1739
The Secretary's Secret #1774

Silhouette Intimate Moments

Running on Empty #1342
Out of Sight #1398

MICHELLE CELMER

Michelle Celmer lives in a southeastern Michigan zoo.

Well, okay, it's really a house, but with three kids (two of them teenagers and all three musicians), three dogs ranging from seventy to ninety pounds each, three cats (two long-haired) and a fifty-gallon tank full of various marine life, sometimes it feels like a zoo. It's rarely quiet, seldom clean, and between after-school jobs, various extracurricular activities and band practice, getting everyone home at the same to share a meal is next to impossible.

You can often find Michelle locked in her office, writing her heart out and loving the fact that she doesn't have to leave the house to go to work, or even change out of her pajamas.

Michelle *loves* to hear from her readers. Drop her a line at: P.O. BOX 300, Clawson, MI 48017, or visit her Web site at: www.michellecelmer.com.

This book is in honor of the dedicated volunteers at Regap of Michigan (Retired Greyhounds as Pets), www.rescuedgreyhound.org.

It has been a pleasure and a privilege to be a part of something so special

One

Nick Bateman lay in bed in the honeymoon suite of the hotel, pretending to be asleep, wondering what the hell he'd just done.

Instead of spending his wedding night with the woman who was supposed to be his new wife—the one he'd left at the altar halfway through their vows—he'd slept with Zoë, his office manager.

He would have liked to blame the champagne for what had happened, but two shared bottles wasn't exactly enough to get him rip roaring drunk. He'd been too intoxicated to drive, no question, but sober enough to know it was a really bad idea to sleep with an employee.

And even worse, he considered Zoë one of his best friends.

He rubbed a hand across the opposite side of the mattress and could feel lingering traces of heat. The scent of sex and pheromones and her spicy perfume clung to his skin and the sheets.

He heard a thump and a softly muttered curse from somewhere across the room. She had been slinking through the darkness for several minutes now, probably looking for her clothes.

His only excuse for what he'd let happen, even if it was a lame one, was that on the night of his failed wedding he'd been discouraged and depressed and obviously not thinking straight.

Instead of saying *I do*, he'd said *I don't* and skipped out on his fiancée. His second, in fact. Could he help it if it had only occurred to him just then the terrible mistake he was making? That his desire for a wife and family was clouding his judgment? That after a month of courtship he barely knew the woman standing beside him, and she was in fact—as his friends had tried to warn him—only after his money.

What a nightmare.

He would never forget the look of stunned indignation on Lynn's face when, halfway through their vows, he had turned to her and said, "I'm sorry, I can't do this." He could still feel the sting of her fist where it had connected solidly with his jaw.

He'd deserved it. Despite being a lying, blood-sucking vampire, she didn't deserve to be humiliated that way. Why was it that he couldn't seem to find the right woman? It had been five years since he decided he was ready to settle down. He'd figured by now he would be happily married with at least one baby and another on the way.

Nothing in his life was going the way it was supposed to. The way he'd planned.

After the abrupt end of the service, Zoë had driven him to the hotel where the honeymoon suite awaited and the champagne was already chilling. He'd been in no mood to drink alone, so he'd invited her in. She'd ordered room service— even though he hadn't been particularly hungry—and made him an ice pack for his jaw.

She always took care of him. And damn, had she taken care of him last night.

He wasn't even sure how it started. One minute they were sitting there talking, then she gave him this look, and the next thing he knew his tongue was in her mouth and they were tearing each other's clothes off.

Her mouth had been so hot and sweet, her body soft and warm and responsive. And the sex? It had been freaking fantastic. He'd never been with a woman quite so...*vocal* in bed. He'd never once had to guess what she wanted because she wasn't shy about asking.

God, he'd really slept with Zoë.

It's not that he'd never looked at her in a sexual way. He'd always been attracted to her. She wasn't the kind of woman who hypnotized a man with her dazzling good looks—not that she wasn't pretty—but Zoë's beauty was subtle. It came from the inside, from her quirky personality and strength.

But there were some lines you just didn't cross. The quickest way for a man to ruin a friendship with a woman was to have sex with her.

He knew this from experience.

Thankfully, he hadn't done irrevocable damage. As much as he wanted a family, Zoë wanted to stay single and childless just as badly. Unlike other female employees he'd made the mistake of sleeping with—back when he was still young, arrogant and monumentally stupid—she wouldn't expect or want a commitment.

Which was a *good* thing, right?

There was another thump, and what sounded like a gasp of pain, right beside the bed this time. He had two choices, he could continue to pretend he was asleep and let her stumble around in the dark, or he could face what they had done.

He reached over and switched on the lamp, squinting against the sudden bright light, both surprised and pleased to find a completely bare, shapely rear end not twelve inches from his face.

Zoë Simmons let out a shriek and swung around, blinking against the harsh light, clutching her crumpled dress to her bare breasts. This was like the dream she frequently had where she was walking through the grocery store naked. Only this was worse, because she was awake.

And honestly, right now, she would rather be caught naked in a room full of strangers than with Nick.

"You scared me," she admonished. So much for sneaking out before he woke up. Call her a chicken, but she hadn't been ready to face what they'd done. How many times they had done it.

How many different positions they had done it in...

The bed was in shambles and there were discarded condom wrappers on the bedside table and floor. She winced when she thought of the way they'd touched each other, the places they had touched. How incredibly, shockingly, mind-meltingly *fantastic* it had been.

And how it could never, *ever* happen again.

"Going somewhere?" he asked.

"'Fraid so."

He looked over at the digital clock beside the bed. "It's the middle of the night."

Exactly.

"I thought it would be best if I leave." But God help her, he wasn't making it easy. He sat there naked from the waist up, looking like a Greek god, a picture of bulging muscle and golden skin, and all she wanted to do was climb back into bed with him.

No. *Bad* Zoë.

This had to end, and it had to end *now*.

She edged toward the bathroom, snagging her purse from the floor. "I'm going to go get dressed, then we'll...talk."

She backed into the bathroom, his eyes never

leaving her face. She shut and locked the door, then switched on the light, saw her reflection and let out a sound that ranked somewhere between a horrified gasp and a gurgle of surprise.

Just when she thought this night couldn't get any worse.

Her hair was smashed flat on one side of her head and sticking up on the other, last night's eyeliner was smeared under her red, puffy eyes, and she had pillow indentations all over her left cheek. Unlike Nick who woke up looking like a Playgirl centerfold. It's a miracle he hadn't run screaming from the room when he saw her.

Had there been a window in the bathroom, she would have climbed through it.

She splashed water on her face, used a tissue to wipe away the smudges under her eyes, then dug through her purse for a hair band. Finger combing her hair with damp hands, she pulled it taut and fastened it into a ponytail. She had no clue where her bra and panties had disappeared to, and there was no way in hell she was going to go hunting for them. She would just have to go commando until she got home.

She tugged on her battered dress, smoothing out the wrinkles as best she could. In his haste to undress her, Nick had torn one of the spaghetti straps loose. One side of the bodice hung dangerously low. The form-fitting silk skirt was still a little damp and stained from the glass of champagne she'd spilled on herself.

It was the dress she'd worn to both of Nick's weddings. It looked as if maybe it was time to retire it.

Or incinerate it.

Zoë studied her reflection, hiking the bodice up over her half exposed breast. Not great, but passable. Maybe everyone wouldn't look at her and automatically think, *tramp*, as she traipsed through the five-star hotel lobby. Not that she would run into too many people at three-thirty in the morning.

She heard movement from the other room, and fearing she would catch him as naked and exposed as he had caught her —she cringed at the thought of her big rear end in his face when he turned the light on—she called, "I'm coming out now!"

When he didn't respond, she unlocked the door and edged it open, peeking out. He sat on the bed wearing only the slacks from last night, his chest bare.

And boy what a chest it was. It's not as if she'd never seen it before. But after touching it…and oh my, was that a bite mark on his left shoulder? She also seemed to recall giving him a hickey somewhere south of his belt, not to mention the other things she'd done with her mouth…

Shame seared her inside and out. What had they done?

As she stepped toward him, she noticed the gaping hole in the front of his pants. She was about to point out that the barn door was open, then remembered that in her haste to get his slacks off last night, she'd broken the zipper. They'd torn at each other's clothes, unable to get naked fast enough, as if they'd been working up to that moment for ten long years and couldn't bear to wait a second longer. She would never forget the way he'd plunged inside her, hard and fast and deep. The way she'd wrapped her legs around his hips and ground herself against him, how she'd moaned and begged for more…

Oh God, what had they done?

She clutched her purse to her chest, searching the floor for her shoes. She needed to get out of there pronto, before she did something even stupider, like whip her dress off and jump him.

"I think these belong to you." Nick was holding up her black lace bra and matching thong. "I found them under the covers."

Swell.

"Thanks." She snatched them from him and stuffed both in her tiny purse.

"Should we talk about this?" he asked.

"If it's all the same to you, I'd rather leave and pretend it never happened."

He raked a hand through his short blue-black hair. Thick dark stubble shadowed his jaw, which explained the chafing on her inner thighs.

"That is one way to handle it," he said, sounding almost disappointed.

He had to know as well as she did that this was a fluke. It never should have happened. And it sure as hell would never, *ever* happen again.

Not that he was a bad guy. Nick was rich,

gorgeous and genuinely nice—and okay, a touch stubborn and overbearing at times. And there were occasional moments when she wanted to smack him upside the head. But he was sweet when he wanted to be and generous to a fault.

How he hadn't found the right woman yet, she would never understand. Maybe he was just trying too hard. Either that or he had really bad luck. When it came to finding the wrong woman, he was like a magnet.

Personally, she liked her life just the way it was. No commitments. No accountability to anyone but herself and Dexter, her cat. She'd already done the mommy-caregiver gig back home. While both her parents worked full time jobs she'd been responsible for her eight younger brothers and sisters. All Nick had talked about during the past five years was marrying Susie homemaker and having a brood of children. The closest she was going to get to a diaper was in the grocery store, and that was only because it was across the aisle from the cat food.

The day Zoë turned eighteen she'd run like hell, clear across Michigan, from Petoskey to Detroit. And if it hadn't been for Nick, she wouldn't have lasted a month on her own. Despite having just started his construction company, or maybe because of it, he hadn't fired her when he found out she'd lied on her application about having office experience.

The truth was, she couldn't even type and her phone skills were questionable. Instead of kicking her out the door, which she admittedly deserved, his alpha male gene had gone into overdrive and he'd set out to save her. He'd helped put her through college, trained her in the business—in life. She'd been more than a tad sheltered and naïve.

To this day Zoë didn't know why he'd been so good to her, why he'd taken her under his wing. When they met, something just clicked.

And, in turn, Zoë had been Nick's only family. The only person he could depend on. He never seemed to expect or want more than that.

No way she would throw it all away on one stupid lapse in judgment, because the truth of the matter was, in a relationship, they wouldn't last. They were too different.

They would kill each other the first week.

"We've obviously made a big mistake," she said. She spotted her brand new Jimmy Choo pumps peeking out from under the bed. She used her big toe to drag them out and shoved her feet in. "We've known each other a long time. I'd hate to see our friendship, our working relationship, screwed up because of this."

"That would suck," he agreed. He sure was taking this well. Not that she'd expected him to be upset. But he didn't have to be so…*agreeable*. He could at least pretend he was sorry it wouldn't happen again.

She hooked a thumb over her shoulder. "I'm going to go now."

He pulled himself to his feet. She was wearing three-inch heels and he was still a head taller. "I'll drive you home."

She held up a hand to stop him. "No, no. That's not necessary. I'll call a cab."

He looked down at the clock. "It's after three."

All the more reason not to let him drive her home. In the middle of the night she felt less…accountable. What if, when they got there, she invited him in? She didn't want him getting the wrong idea, and she wasn't sure if she could trust herself.

Astonishing what a night of incredible sex could do to cloud a girl's judgment. "I'd really rather you didn't. I'll be fine, honest."

"Then take my truck," he said, taking her hand and pressing his keys into it. "I'll catch a cab in the morning."

"You're sure?"

"I'm sure."

He gestured toward the bedroom door and followed her into the dark sitting room. When they got to the door she turned to face him. The light from the bedroom illuminated the right side of his face. The side with the dimple.

But he wasn't smiling. He looked almost sad.

Well, duh, he'd just split up with his fiancée. Of course he was sad.

"I'm really sorry about what happened with Lynn. You'll meet someone else, I promise." Someone unlike fiancée number one, who informed him on their wedding day that she'd decided to put off having kids for ten years so she could focus on her career. Or fiancée number two who'd been a real prize. Lynn had obviously been after Nick's money, but he'd been so desperate to satisfy his driving need to procreate, he'd been blind to what he was getting himself into. Thank goodness he'd come to his senses, let himself see her for what she was.

"I know I will," he said.

"This probably goes without saying, but it would be best if we kept what happened to ourselves. Things could get weird around the office if anyone found out."

"Okay," he agreed. "Not a word."

Huh. That was easy.

Almost *too* easy.

"Well, I should go." She hooked her purse over her shoulder and reached for the doorknob. "I guess I'll see you at work Monday."

He leaned forward and propped a hand above her head on the door, so she couldn't pull it open. "Since this isn't going to happen again, how about one last kiss?"

Oh no, *bad* idea. Nick's kiss is what had gotten them into this mess in the first place. The man could work miracles with his mouth. Had he been a lousy kisser, she never would have slept with him. "I don't think that would be a good idea."

He was giving her that look again, that heavy-lidded hungry look he'd had just before they had attacked each other the first time. And suddenly he seemed to be standing a lot closer. And he smelled so good, *looked* so good in the pale light that her head felt a little swimmy.

"Come on," he coaxed, "one little kiss."

Like a magnet she felt drawn to him. She could feel herself leaning forward even as she told him, "That would be a bad idea."

"Probably," he agreed, easing in to meet her halfway. He caressed her cheek with the tips of his fingers, combed them gently through her hair. The hair band pulled loose and a riot of blond curls sprang free, hanging in damp ringlets around her face.

"Nick, don't," she said. But she didn't do anything to stop him. "We agreed this wouldn't happen again."

"Did we?" His hand slipped down to her shoulder. She felt a tug, and heard the snap of her other spaghetti strap being torn. Her dress was now officially strapless. And in another second it would be lying on the floor.

Oh God, here we go again.

Nick pushed the strap of her purse off the opposite shoulder and it landed with a soft thump on the floor at their feet and his truck keys landed beside it. "We're already here, the damage has been done. Is one more time really going to make that much of a difference?"

It was hard to argue with logic like that, especially when he was nibbling her ear. And he was right. The damage had already been done.

What difference could one more time possibly make?

"Just a quick one," she said, reaching for the fastener on his slacks. She tugged it free and shoved them down his hips. "As long as we agree that what goes on in this room stays in this room."

His lips brushed her shoulder and her knees went weak. "Agreed."

Then he kissed her and she melted.

One more time, she promised herself as he bunched the skirt of her dress up around her waist and lifted her off the floor.

"One more time," she murmured as she locked her legs around his hips and he pinned her body to the wall, entered her with one deep, penetrating thrust.

One more time and they would forget this ever happened...

Two

What difference could one more time *possibly* make? Apparently, more than either she or Nick had anticipated.

Zoë glanced up at the clock above her desk, then down to the bottom drawer of the file cabinet where she'd stashed the bag from the pharmacy behind the employment records. The bag that had been sitting there for four days now because she conveniently kept forgetting to bring it home every night after work. Mostly because she'd been trying to convince herself that she was probably overreacting. She was most likely suffering some funky virus that would clear up on its own. A virus that just happened to zap all of her energy, made her queasy every morning when she rolled out of bed and made her breasts swollen and sore.

And, oh yeah, made her period late.

She was sure there had to be a virus like that, because there was no chance in hell this condition was actually something that would require 2 a.m. feedings and diapers.

She would have a much easier time explaining this away if she wasn't ninety-nine percent sure Nick hadn't been wearing a condom that last time up against the hotel room wall.

It's not as if she could come right out and ask him. Not without him freaking out and things getting really complicated. It had taken several weeks to get past the post-coital weirdness. At first, it had been hard to look him in the eye, knowing he'd seen her naked, had touched her intimately.

Every time she looked at his hands, she remembered the way they felt against her skin. Rough and calloused, but oh so tender. And so big they seemed to swallow up every part of her that he touched.

His slim hips reminded her of the way she'd locked her legs around him as he'd pinned her to the wall. The way he'd entered her, swift and deep. How she'd come apart in his arms.

And his mouth. That wonderfully sinful mouth that melted her like butter in a hot skillet…

No. No. *No.*

Bad Zoë.

She shook away the lingering memory of his lean,

muscular body, of his weight sinking her into the mattress, her body shuddering with pleasure. She'd promised herself at least a hundred times a day that she wasn't going to think about that anymore. Finally things seemed to be getting back to normal. She and Nick could have a conversation without that undertone of awkwardness.

Zoë didn't want to risk rocking the boat.

She hadn't even told her sister Faith, and they told each other almost everything. Although, after their last phone conversation Zoë was under the distinct impression Faith knew something was up. It wouldn't be unlike her sister to drop everything and show up unannounced if she thought there was something that Zoë wasn't telling her.

She took a deep, fortifying breath. She was being ridiculous. She should just take the damned test and get it over with. She'd spent the ten bucks, after all. She might as well get her money's worth. Waiting yet another week wouldn't change the final outcome. Either she was or she wasn't. It would be good to know now, so she could decide what to do.

And decide what she would tell Nick.

As she was reaching for the bottom drawer handle, Shannon from accounting appeared in the doorway and Zoë breathed a sigh of relief.

"Hey, hon, you up for lunch with the girls? We're heading over to Shooters."

Despite being a nervous wreck, she was starving. Though she normally ate a salad for lunch, she would sell her soul for a burger and fries and a gigantic milkshake. And for dessert, a double chocolate sundae. Hold the pickles.

"Lunch sounds wonderful."

She grabbed her purse and jacket and gave the file cabinet one last glance before she followed Shannon into the hall.

As soon as she got back from lunch, she promised herself. She would put the test in her purse so she wouldn't forget it, and tonight when she got home she would get to the bottom of this.

Nick walked down the hall to Zoë's office and popped his head inside, finding it empty and feeling a screwy mix of relief and disappointment. He'd come to her office now, knowing she would probably be on her lunch break. Though they'd promised to pretend it hadn't happened, he couldn't seem to make himself forget every erotic detail of their night together. He'd been doing his best to pretend nothing had changed, but something was still a little…*off*.

Something about Zoë—a thing he couldn't quite put his finger on—seemed different.

He couldn't stop himself from wondering, *what if*? What if he'd told her he didn't want to pretend like it hadn't happened?

He just wasn't sure if that's what he really wanted. Were he and Zoë too different for that kind of relationship?

She was a cat person and he had a dog. He was

faded Levi's and worn leather and she was so prim and...*girly*. His music preferences ranged from classic rock to rich, earthy blues with a little jazz piano thrown in for flavor. Zoë seemed to sway toward eighties pop and any female singer, and she had the annoying habit of blaring Christmas music in July.

He was a meat and potatoes man, and as far as he could tell, Zoë existed on salads and bottled mineral water. He watched reality television and ESPN and she preferred crime dramas and chick flicks.

In fact, he couldn't think of a single thing they had in common. Besides the sex, which frankly they did pretty damned well.

Even if they could get past all of their differences, there was the problem of them wanting completely different things from life. In all the years he'd known her, she'd never once expressed a desire to have children. Not that he could blame her given her family history. But he'd grown up an only child raised by an aunt and uncle who'd had no use for the eight-year-old bastard dumped in their care. He'd spent his childhood in boarding schools and camps.

He wanted a family—at least three kids, maybe more. He just had to find a woman who wanted that, too. One who wasn't more interested in climbing the corporate ladder than having a family. And definitely one who wouldn't insist on a two week European honeymoon followed by mansion hunting in one of Detroit's most exclusive communities.

Material things didn't mean much to him. He was

content with his modest condo and modest vehicle. His modest life. All the money in the world didn't buy happiness. Thousands of dollars in gifts from his aunt and uncle had never made up for a lack of love and affection. His children would always know they were loved. They would never be made to feel like an inconvenience. And he sure as hell would never abandon them.

It had taken him years to realize there wasn't anything wrong with him. That he didn't drive people away. With a long history of mental illness, his mother could barely take care of herself much less a child, and his aunt and uncle simply had no interest in being parents. It would have been easy for them to hand him back over to social services when his mom lost custody. At least they'd taken responsibility for him.

If not for the lack of affection, one might even say he'd been spoiled as a kid. If he wanted or needed something all it took was a phone call to his uncle and it was his.

A convertible sports car the day he got his driver's license? No problem.

An all-expenses-paid trip to Cancún for graduation? It's yours.

The best education money can buy at a first-rate East Coast school? Absolutely.

But no one had handed him his education. He'd worked his tail off to make the dean's list every semester, to graduate at the top of his class. To make his aunt and uncle proud, even if they didn't know how to show it. And when he'd asked his uncle to loan him the money to start his company, the entire astronomical sum had been wired to his account within twenty-four hours.

They wouldn't win any awards for parents of the year, but his aunt and uncle had done the best they could.

He would do better.

There had to be a Ms. Right out there just waiting for him to sweep her off her feet. A woman who wanted the same things he did. And hopefully he would find her before he was too old to play ball with his son, to teach his daughter to Rollerblade.

He stepped into Zoë's office, trying to remember where in the file cabinet she kept the personnel files. Seeing as how she wasn't exactly organized, they could be pretty much anywhere.

Despite the disarray, she somehow managed to keep the office running like a finely tuned watch. She'd become indispensable. He would be lost without her.

He started at the top and worked his way down, finding them, of course, in the bottom drawer. He located the file of a new employee, Mark O'Connell, to see if there was some reason why the guy would be missing so much work. Not to mention showing up late. Nick was particular when he hired new employees. He didn't understand how someone with such impeccable references could be so unpredictable on the job.

He grabbed the file and was about to shut the

drawer when he saw the edge of a brown paper bag poking up from the back.

Huh. What could that be? He didn't remember seeing that the last time he looked in here.

He grabbed the bag and pulled it out. He was about to peek inside, when behind him he heard a gasp.

"What are you doing?"

Nick turned, the pharmacy bag in his hand, and Zoë stood in the office doorway, back from lunch, frozen. If he opened that bag, things were going to get really complicated really fast.

"I found this in the file cabinet," he said.

When she finally found her voice, she did her best to keep it calm and rational. Freaking out would only make things worse. "I don't appreciate you going through my things."

He gave her an annoyed look. "How was I supposed to know it's yours? It was in the file cabinet with the personnel files. The files I need to have access to, to run my company."

He was right. She should have kept it in her car, or her purse. Of course, then what excuse would she have had for not using it? She walked toward him and held out a hand. "You're right, I apologize. Can I have it back please?"

He looked at her, then at the bag. "What is it?"

"Something personal."

She took another step toward him, hand outstretched, and he took a step back.

A devious grin curled his lips, showing off the dent in his right cheek. "How much is it worth to you?"

He hadn't teased her in weeks. Now was not the time to start acting like his pain-in-the-behind old self. "That isn't funny, Nick. Give it to me."

He held the bag behind his back. "Make me."

How could a grown man act so damned juvenile? He didn't have kids, so what, he'd act like one?

She stepped toward him, her temper flaring, and held out her hand. "*Please.*"

He sidestepped out of her way, around her desk, thoroughly enjoying himself if his goofy grin was any indication.

She felt like punching him.

Couldn't he see that she was fuming mad? Didn't he care that he was upsetting her?

Heat climbed up her throat and into her cheeks. "You're acting like an ass, Nick. Give it back to me *now.*"

The angrier she became, the more amused he looked. "Must be something pretty important to get your panties in such a twist," he teased, clasping the bag with two fingers and swinging it just out of her reach. Why did he have to be so darned tall? "If you want it so badly, come and get it."

She slung her hands up in defeat. "Fine, look if you have to. If you find tampons so thoroughly interesting."

Tampons. Didn't she wish.

He raised a brow at her, as if he wasn't sure he should believe her or not. As he lowered the bag, uncurling the edge to take a peek, she lunged for him. Her fingers skimmed the bag and he jerked his arm back, inadvertently flinging the test box out. In slow motion it spiraled across the room, hit the wall with a smack and landed label side up on the carpet.

Uh-oh.

For several long seconds time seemed to stand still, then it surged forward with a force that nearly gave her whiplash.

Nick looked at the box, then at her, then back at the box and all the amusement evaporated from his face. "What the hell is this?"

She closed her eyes. Damn, damn, damn.

"Zoë?"

She opened her eyes and glared at him. "What, you can't read?"

She grabbed the bag from his slack fingers then marched over and snatched the box from the floor.

"Zoë, do you think you're—"

"Of course not!" More like, God, she hoped not.

"Are you late?"

She gave him a *duh* look.

"Of course you are, or you wouldn't need the test." He raked a hand through his hair. "How late are you exactly?"

"I'm just a little late. I'm sure it's nothing."

"We slept together over a month ago. How late is a *little* late?"

She shrugged. "Two weeks, maybe three."

"Which is it, two or three?"

Oh, hell. She slumped into her desk chair. "Probably closer to three."

He took a long deep breath and blew it out. She could tell he was fighting to stay calm. "And why am I just hearing about this now?"

"I thought maybe it was a virus or an infection or something," she said, and he gave her an incredulous look. "I was in *denial,* okay?"

"Missed periods can happen for lots of reasons, right? Like stress?"

She flicked her thumbnail nervously back and forth, fraying the edge of the box. Stressed? Who me? "Sure, I guess."

"Besides, we used protection."

"Did we?"

He shot back an indignant, "You know we did."

She felt a glimmer of hope. Condoms could fail, but the odds were slim. Maybe she really wasn't pregnant. Maybe this was all in her head. "Even the last time?"

There was a pause, then he asked, "The last time?"

Suddenly he didn't sound so confident. Suddenly he had an, *Oh-damn-what-have-I-done?* look on his face.

Her stomach began to slither down from her abdomen. "You know, against the wall, by the door. We used a condom then too, right?" she asked hopefully, as if wishing it were true would actually make it true.

He scratched the coarse stubble on his chin. The guy could shave ten times a day but he was so dark he almost always had a five o'clock shadow. "Honestly, I can't remember."

Oh, this was not good. She could feel her control slipping, panic squeezing the air from her lungs. "You can't *remember?*"

He sat on the corner of her desk. "Apparently, you can't either."

He was right. That wasn't fair. This was in no way his fault. "I'm sorry. I'm just...edgy."

"If I had to guess, I would say that since I have no memory of using one, and my wallet was in the other room, we probably didn't."

At least he was being honest. Obviously they had both been too swept away by passion to think about contraceptives. But that had been what, their fourth time? Didn't a man's body take a certain amount of time to...*reinforce the troops.* Were there even any little swimmers left by then?

Leave it to her to have unprotected sex with a guy who had super sperm.

"I guess there's only one way to find out for sure," he said. "Taking the test here would probably be a bad idea, seeing as how anyone could walk into the bathroom. So would you be more comfortable taking it at your place or mine?"

This was really happening. With *Nick* of all people.

When she didn't answer right away he asked, "Or is this something you need to be alone for?"

Being alone was the last thing she wanted. They were in this together. She didn't doubt for an instant that he would be there for her, whatever the outcome. "We'll do it at my house."

He rose to his feet. "Okay, let's go."

Her eyes went wide. "You want to go *now?* It's the middle of the workday."

"It's not like we're going to get fired. I own the company. Besides, you know what they say."

She thought about it for a second then said, "Curiosity killed the cat?"

He grinned. "There's no time like the present."

Three

Nick drove them the ten minutes to Zoë's house in Birmingham. They didn't say much. What could they say? Zoë spent the majority of her time praying, Please, God, let it be negative.

How had she gotten herself into this mess?

Her devout Catholic parents still believed that at the age of twenty-eight she was as pure as the driven snow. If the test was positive, what would she tell them? Well, Mom and Dad, I was snow-white, but I drifted.

They were going to kill her. Or disown her.

Or both.

And this would surely be enough to send her fragile, ailing grandmother hurtling through death's door. She would instantly be labeled the family black sheep.

It didn't matter that her parents had been nagging her to settle down for years.

When are you going to find a nice man? When are you going to have babies?

How about never?

And if the man she settled down with was Nick they would be ecstatic. Despite the fact that he wasn't Catholic, they adored him. Since the first time she'd brought him home for Thanksgiving dinner they'd adopted him into the fold. And Nick had been swept up into the total chaos and craziness that was her family. He loved it almost as much as it drove her nuts.

So, if she were to call home and tell them she and Nick were getting hitched, she'd be daughter of the year. But the premarital sex thing would still be a major issue. In her parents' eyes, what they had done was a sin.

She let her head fall back against the seat and closed her eyes. Maybe this was just a bad dream. Maybe all she needed to do was pinch herself real hard and she would wake up.

She caught a hunk of skin between her thumb and forefinger, the fleshy part under her upper arm that the self-defense people claim is the most sensitive, and gave it a good hard squeeze.

"Ow!"

"What's wrong?"

She opened her eyes and looked around. Still in Nick's monster truck, rumbling down the street, and he was shooting her a concerned look.

She sighed. So much for her dream theory.

"Nothing. I'm just swell," she said, turning to look out the window, barely seeing the houses of her street whizzing past.

"Don't get upset until we know for sure," he said, but she was pretty sure he, like her, already knew what the result would be. They'd had unprotected sex and her period was late. The test was going to be positive.

She was going to have Nick's baby.

When they got to her house, he took her keys from her and opened the door. He'd been inside her house a thousand times, but today it felt so…*surreal*. As if she'd stepped onto the set of film.

A horror film.

She and Nick were the stars, and any second some lunatic was going to pop out of the kitchen wielding a knife and hack them to pieces.

She slipped her jacket off and tossed it over the back of the couch while Nick took in her cluttered living room.

Last night's dinner dishes still sat on the coffee table, the plate covered with little kitty lick marks from Dexter her cat. Newspapers from the past two weeks lay in a messy pile at one end of the couch.

She looked down at the rug, at the tufts of white cat fur poking out from the Berber and realized it had been too long since she'd last vacuumed. Her entire house—entire life—was more than a little chaotic right now. As if acting irresponsibly would somehow prove what a lousy parent she would be.

Nick looked around and made a face. "You really need to hire a maid."

She tossed her purse down on the cluttered coffee table. "I am *so* not in the mood for a lecture on my domestic shortcomings."

He had the decency to look apologetic.

"Sorry." He reached inside his leather bomber jacket and pulled out the test kit. "I guess we should just get this over with, huh?"

"We?" Like he had to go in the bathroom and pee on a stick. Like he had to endure months of torture if it was positive. A guy like him wouldn't last a week on the nest. He may have been tough, may have been able to bench press a compact car, but five minutes of hard labor and he would be toast.

Her mother had done home births for Zoë's three youngest siblings and Zoë had had the misfortune of being stuck in the room with her for the last one. She had witnessed the horror. Going through it once seemed like torture enough, but understandable since most women probably didn't realize what they were getting themselves into. But *nine* times. That was just crazy.

"I'm afraid to go in there," she said.

Nick reached up and dropped one big, work-roughened hand on her shoulder, giving it a gentle squeeze. "We're in this together, Zoë. Whatever the outcome. We'll get through it."

It amazed her at times, how such a big, burly guy who oozed testosterone could be so damned tender and sweet. Not that the stubborn, overbearing alpha male gene had passed him by. He could be a major pain in the behind, too. But he'd never let her down in a time of need and she didn't believe for a second that he would now.

"Okay, here goes." She took the test kit from him and walked to the bathroom, closing and locking the door behind her, her stomach tangled in knots. She opened the box and with a trembling hand spilled the contents out onto the vanity.

"Please, God," she whispered, "let it be negative."

She read the instructions three times, just to be sure she was doing it right, then followed them word for word. It was amazingly quick and simple for such a life-altering procedure. *Too simple.*

Less than five minutes later, after rereading the instructions one more time just to be sure, she had her answer.

Nick paced the living room rug, his eye on the bathroom door, wondering what in the heck was taking Zoë so long. She'd been in there almost twenty minutes now and he hadn't heard a peep out of her. No curdling screams, no thud to indicate she'd hit the floor in a dead faint. And no whoops of joy.

It was ironic that not five minutes before she stepped into her office he'd been thinking about having children. Just not with her, and not quite so soon. Ideally he would like to be married, but life had a way of throwing a curve ball.

At least, his life did.

He let out a thundering sneeze and glanced with disdain at the fluffy white ball of fur sunbathing on the front windowsill. It stared back at him with scornful green eyes.

He was so not a cat person.

He sat on the couch, propped his elbows on his knees and rested his chin on his fisted hands.

So what if she was pregnant?

The truth was, this was all happening so fast, he wasn't sure how he felt about it. What he did know is that if she didn't come out of the damned bathroom soon, he was going to pound the door down. It couldn't possibly take this long. He remembered the box specifically stating something about results in only minutes.

As if conjuring her through sheer will, the bathroom door swung open and Zoë stepped out. Nick shot to his feet. He didn't have to ask what the results were, he could see it in her waxy, pasty-white pallor. Her wide, glassy-eyed disbelief.

"Oh boy," he breathed. Zoë was pregnant.

He was going to be a father. They were going to be parents.

Together.

She looked about two seconds from passing out cold, so he walked over to where she stood and pulled her into his arms. She collapsed against him, her entire body trembling.

She rested her forehead on his chest, wrapped her

arms around him, and he buried his nose in her hair. She smelled spicy and sweet, like cinnamon and apples. He realized, he'd missed this. Since that night in the hotel, he'd been itching to get his arms around her again.

He'd almost forgotten just how good it felt to be close to her, how perfectly she fit in his arms. Something had definitely changed between them that night in the hotel. Something that he doubted would ever change back.

For a while they only held each other, until she'd stopped shaking and she wasn't breathing so hard. Until she had gone from cold and rigid to warm and relaxed in his arms.

He cupped her chin and tilted her face up. "It's going to be okay."

"What are we going to do?" she asked.

"Well, I guess we're going to have a baby," he said, and felt the corners of his mouth begin to tip up.

Zoë gaped at him, her look going from bewilderment to abject horror. She broke from his grasp and took a step back. "Oh my God."

"What?"

"You're smiling. You're *happy* about this."

Was he?

The smile spread to encompass his entire face. He tried to stop it, then realized it was impossible. He really *was* happy. For five years now he'd felt it was time to settle down and start a family. True, this wasn't exactly how he planned it, and he sure as hell hadn't planned on doing it with Zoë, but that didn't mean it wouldn't work. That didn't mean they shouldn't at least give it a shot.

He gave her a shrug. "Yeah, I guess I am. Would you feel better if I was angry?"

"Of course not. But do you have even the slightest clue what we're getting into? What *I'll* have to go through?"

She made it sound as though he was making her remove an appendage. "You're having a baby, Zoë. It's not as if it's never been done before."

"Of course it has, but have you ever actually witnessed a baby being born?"

No, but he definitely wanted to be in the delivery room. He wouldn't miss that for anything. "I'm sure it will be fascinating."

"*Fascinating*? I was there when my mom had Jonah, my youngest brother."

"And?"

"Have you ever seen the movie, *The Thing?*" she asked, and he nodded. "You remember the scene where the alien bursts out of the guy and there is this huge spray of blood and guts? Well, it's kinda' like that. Only it goes on for *hours*. And hurts twice as much.

"And that's only the beginning," she went on, in full rant. "After it's born there are sleepless nights to look forward to and endless dirty diapers. Never having a second to yourself…a *moment's* silence. They cry and whine and demand and smother. Not to mention that they cost a fortune. Then they get older and there's school and homework and rebellion. It never ends. They're yours to worry about and pull your hair out over until the day you *die*."

Wow. He knew she was jaded by her past, but he'd never expected her to be this traumatized.

"Zoë, you were just a kid when you had to take care of your brothers and sisters. It wasn't fair for your parents to burden you with that much responsibility." He rubbed a hand down her arm, trying to get her to relax and see things rationally. "Right now you're still in shock. I know that when you take some time to digest it, you'll be happy."

She closed her eyes and shook her head. "I'm not ready for this. I don't know if I'll *ever* be ready for it."

A startling, disturbing thought occurred to him. What if she didn't want to have the baby? What if she was thinking about terminating the pregnancy? It was her body so, of course, the choice was up to her, but he'd do whatever he could to talk her out of it, to rationalize with her.

"Are you saying you don't want to have the baby?" he asked.

She looked up at him, confused. "It's not like I have a choice."

"Every woman has a choice, Zoë."

She gave him another one of those horrified looks and folded a hand protectively over her stomach. He didn't think she even realized she was doing it. "I'm not going to get rid of it if that's what you mean. What kind of person do you think I am?"

Thankfully, not that kind. "I've never considered raising a baby on my own, but I will if that's what you want."

"Of course that's not what I want! I could never give a baby up. Once you have it, it's yours. My brothers and sisters may have driven me crazy but I love them to death. I wouldn't trade them in for anything."

He rubbed a hand across the stubble on his jaw. "You're confusing the hell out of me."

"I'm keeping the baby," she said firmly. "I'm just...I guess I'm still in shock. This was not a part of my master plan. And you're the last man on earth I saw myself doing it with. No offense."

"None taken." How could he be offended when he'd been thinking the same thing earlier. Although maybe not the *last on earth* part.

She walked over to the couch and crumpled onto the cushions. "My parents are going to kill me. They think I'm still a good Catholic girl. A twenty-eight-year-old, snow-white virgin who goes to church twice a week. What am I going to tell them?"

Nick sat down beside her. He slipped an arm around her shoulder and she leaned into him, soft and warm.

Yeah, this was nice. It felt...right.

And just like that he knew exactly what he needed to do.

"I guess you only have one choice," he said.

"Live the rest of my life in shame?"

Her pessimism made him grin. "No. I think you should marry me."

* * *

Zoë pulled out of Nick's arms and stared up at him. "Marry you? Are you *crazy?*"

Dumb question, Zoë. Of course he was crazy.

Rather than being angry with her, he smiled, as if he'd been expecting her to question his sanity. "What's so crazy about it?"

If he couldn't figure that out himself, he really was nuts.

"If we get married right away, your parents don't have to know you were already pregnant. Problem solved."

And he thought marrying someone he didn't love *wouldn't* be a problem? Not that kind of love anyway. She didn't doubt that he loved her as a friend, and she him, but that wasn't enough.

"We're both feeling emotional and confused," she said. He more than her, obviously. "Maybe we should take a day or two to process this before we make any kind of life altering decisions."

"We're having a baby together, Zoë. You don't get much more life altering than that."

"My point exactly. We have a lot to consider."

"Look, I know you're not crazy about the idea of getting married to anyone—"

"And you're *too* crazy about it. Did you even stop to think that you would be marrying me for all the wrong reasons? You want Susie homemaker. Someone to squeeze out your babies, keep your house clean and have dinner waiting in the oven when you get home from work. Well, take a look around you, Nick. My life is in shambles. My house is a disaster and if I can't microwave myself a meal in five minutes or less, I don't buy it."

He didn't look hurt by her refusal, which made her that much more certain marrying him would be a bad idea. She could never be the cardboard cutout wife he was looking for. She wouldn't be any kind of a wife at all.

And even if they could get past all of that, it still wouldn't work. He was such a good guy. Perfect in so many ways. Except the one that counted the most.

He didn't love her.

She took his hand between her two. It was rough and slightly calloused from years of working construction with his employees. He may have owned the company, may have had more money than God, but he liked getting his hands dirty. He liked to feel the sun on his back and fresh air in his lungs. One day cooped up in the office and he was climbing the walls.

She didn't doubt that he would put just as much of himself into his marriage. He was going to make some lucky woman one hell of a good husband.

Just not her.

"It was a noble gesture. But I think we both need to take some time and decide what it is we really want."

"How much time?" he asked.

"I'm going to have to make a doctor's appointment. Let's get through that first then we'll worry about the other stuff."

Who knows, maybe she got a false positive from the pregnancy test. Maybe she would get a blood test at the doctor's office and find out they had done all this worrying for nothing.

Four

"Congratulations! Your test was positive! If you haven't yet made a follow-up appointment with Doctor Gordon, please dial one. If you need to speak to a nurse, dial two—"

Zoë hung up the phone in her office, cutting short the obnoxiously perky prerecorded message she'd gotten when she phoned the doctor's office for her blood test results.

It was official. Not that it hadn't been official before. The blood test had just been a formality. She was definitely, without a doubt, having Nick's baby.

Oh boy.

Or girl, she supposed.

She would walk down to his office and tell him,

but he'd been in her office every ten minutes wondering if she'd made the call.

She looked down at her watch. Why get up when he was due back in another six minutes?

"Well?"

She looked up to find him standing in her doorway watching her expectantly. "You're early."

"Early?" His brow knit into a frown. "Did you call yet?"

"I called."

He stepped into her office and shut the door. "And?"

She sighed. "As my mother used to say, 'I'm in the family way.'"

"Wow." He took deep breath and blew it out. "Are you okay?"

She nodded. She really was. She'd had a few days to think about it, and she was definitely warming to the idea. Not that it wouldn't complicate things. But it wasn't the end of the world either. She would have one kid. She could handle that. "I'm okay."

He walked over to her desk and sat on the edge, facing her. She could see that he was happy, even though he was trying to hide it. And why should he? What normal woman wouldn't want the father of her baby to be excited?

"It's okay to be happy," she told him. "I promise I won't freak out again."

The corners of his mouth quirked up. "I guess this means we have things to discuss."

She knew exactly what *things* he was referring to. He looked so genuinely excited, so happy, she didn't doubt for one second that he would be a wonderful father. But a husband? She wasn't sure if she was ready for one of those. She didn't know if she would *ever* be ready. The idea of sharing her life with someone, all the compromise and sacrifice it would take…it just seemed like a lot to ask. She was happy with her life the way it was.

That didn't mean she couldn't possibly be happier with Nick there, but what if she wasn't?

As promised, he hadn't said a word about marriage while they waited for the test results. Now he looked as if he was ready for an answer.

"It's nothing personal, Nick. I just…I'm afraid it wouldn't work between us."

"Why wouldn't it? We're friends. We work well together. We understand each other." He leaned in closer, his eyes locked on hers. "Not to mention that in the sexual chemistry department we're off the charts."

God, she wished he wouldn't look at her that way. It scrambled her brain. And she hated that he was right. But good sex—even fantastic sex—wasn't enough to make a marriage work.

He leaned in even closer and she could smell traces of his musky aftershave, see the dots of brown in his hazel eyes. "Can you honestly say you haven't thought about that night at least a dozen times a day since it happened?"

"It wasn't *that* good." She tried to sound cocky, but her voice came out warm and soft instead. It had been more like a hundred times a day.

Nick grinned and leaned forward, resting his hands on the arms of her chair, caging her in. "Yes, it was. It was the best sex you ever had. Admit it."

Heat and testosterone rolled off his body in waves, making her feel light-headed and tingly all over. "Okay, yeah, maybe it was. But that's not the point. I don't want to jump into anything we might regret. What if we get married and find out a month later that we drive each other crazy?"

"Too late for that, sweetheart." He reached up and touched her cheek and her heart shimmied in her chest. "You already do drive me crazy."

Right now, he was doing the same to her. He looked as if any second he might kiss her. And though she knew it would be a bad idea, she wanted him to anyway. She didn't even care that anyone in the office could walk in and catch them. It would take ten minutes tops for the news to travel through the entire building. For the rumors to start. That was exactly what they *didn't* need right now.

She just wished he would make up his mind, wished he would either kiss her or back off. When he sat so close, his eyes locked with hers, it was difficult to think straight.

Which is probably the exact reason he was doing it. To throw her off balance. To make her agree to things she wasn't ready for.

"I mean drive each other crazy in a bad way," she said.

"So what would you like to do? Date?"

"I think we're a bit past the dating stage, don't you? Socially we get along fine. It's the living together part that worries me."

That grin was back on his face, dimple and all, which usually meant trouble. "That sounds like the perfect solution."

Funny, but she didn't remember mentioning one. "Which solution is that?"

"We could live together."

Live together? "Like in the same house?"

"Sure. What better way to see if we're compatible."

She'd never had a roommate. Not since she left home, anyway. Back then she'd had to share a room with three of her sisters. Three people borrowing her clothes and using her makeup without asking. Although, she doubted that would be a problem with Nick. Her clothes were way too small for him even if he wanted to borrow them and when it came to wearing makeup, well…she *hoped* he didn't.

To get any privacy back home she'd had to lock herself in the bathroom, which would last only a minute or two before someone was pounding on the door to get in.

But she had two bathrooms if she needed a place to escape. A full on the main floor and a half down in the finished part of the basement. Granted her house was barely a thousand square feet, but how much room could one guy take up?

Unless he was thinking she was going to move in with him. His condo was twice the size of her house, but it was in a high-rise in Royal Oak, with people living on every side.

No one should ever live that close to their neighbors. It was too creepy, knowing people could hear you through the walls. She dreamed of one day owning an old farmhouse with acres and acres of property. She wondered how Nick, a born and bred city boy, would feel about that. Despite how well they knew each other, there were still so many things they *didn't* know. So much they had never talked about.

Things they could definitely learn if they were living together.

"And if we are compatible?" she asked.

"Then you marry me."

"Just like that?"

He nodded. "Just like that."

She hated to admit it, but this made sense in a weird way.

My God, was she actually considering this? The only thing worse than premarital sex in her parents' eyes was living in sin without the sanctity of marriage. Of course, what they didn't know wouldn't hurt them. Right?

"If we were to do this, and I'm not saying we are, but *if* we did, logically, I think it would be best if you move in with me," she said. "Your condo can get by without you. I have a yard and a garden to take care of."

"Fine with me," he agreed.

"And we should probably keep this to ourselves."

"Zoë." He shot her a very unconvincing hurt look. "Are you ashamed of me?"

Yeah, right, like it mattered. When it came to self-confidence, Nick had it in bucket loads.

"You know how the people in this building can be. I'm just not ready to deal with the gossip. Not until we've made a decision."

"Which will be when?"

"You mean like a time limit," she asked, and he nodded. "How about a month? If by then it's not working out, we give it a rest."

He sat back, folded his arms across his chest and gave her an assessing look. "A month, huh?"

A month should be plenty of time to tell if they were compatible. In areas other than friendship. And the bedroom.

"And if after a month we haven't killed each other, what then? We set a date?"

The mere idea triggered a wave of anxiety. Her heart rate jumped and her palms began to sweat. "If we can make it one month living together, I promise to give your proposal very serious thought."

"And hey," he said with a casual shrug. "If nothing else, we can save money on gas driving to work together, so it won't be a total loss."

"How can you be so calm about this?" The idea of him moving in was making her a nervous wreck.

"Because I'm confident that after a month of living together, you'll be dying to marry me."

She hoped he was right. "What makes you so sure?"

A devilish grin curled his mouth. "This does."

He leaned toward her and she knew exactly what he was going to do. He was going to kiss her. She knew, and she didn't do a thing to stop him. The crazy thing was, she *wanted* him to kiss her. She didn't care that it would only confuse things more, or that anyone could walk in and catch them.

He didn't work into it either. He just took charge and dove in for the kill. He slipped a hand behind her head, threading his fingers through her hair, planted his lips on hers and proceeded to kiss her stockings off. Her body went limp and her toes curled in her pumps.

She'd almost forgotten how good a kisser he was, how exciting and warm he tasted. The memory lapse was purely a self-defense mechanism. Otherwise there would have been a lot of kissing going on these past weeks.

She could feel herself sinking deeper under his spell, melting into a squishy puddle in her chair. Her fingers curled in his hair, nails raked his scalp. His big, warm hand cupped the back of her head with gentle but steady pressure, as if he wasn't going to let her get away.

Yeah, right, like she would even try.

Hearing her office door open barely fazed her, nor

did the, "Zoë, I need—*whoops!*" of whomever had come in. Or the loud click of the door closing behind them as they left. And the very real possibility of the news reaching everyone in the building by day's end.

Nick broke the kiss and backed away, gazing down at her with heavy-lidded eyes. "So much for keeping this to ourselves."

"Yeah, oops." She should care that their secret was out—well, at least one of their secrets—but for some reason she didn't. In fact, she was wondering if maybe he should kiss her again. Her cheeks felt warm and her scalp tingled where his hand had been. She was sure if she tried to get up and walk her legs wouldn't work right.

One kiss and she was a wreck.

"So, when do you want me to move in?" he asked, his dimple winking at her.

How about right now? she thought. But she didn't want to sound too eager. Then again it *was* Friday. That would give him all weekend to settle in.

Oh what the heck?

She looked up at him and smiled. "How about tonight?"

There was a reindeer standing on Zoë's front porch.

Nick stood beside it holding the reins in one hand, a duffle bag in the other.

Okay, it was actually a leash he was holding, and the deer was really a dog. A very large, skinny dog with a shiny coat the color of sable.

"What is that?" she asked through the safety of the screen. Did he really think he was bringing that thing into her house?

"This is my dog, Tucker." At her completely blank look he added, "You knew I had one."

Yeah, she knew, but it never occurred to her that it would be moving in, too. "This is going to be a problem. I have a cat."

"Tucker has a low prey drive, so it shouldn't be an issue."

"Prey drive?" She snapped the lock on the storm door. "Dexter is not prey."

"Tucker is a retired racing greyhound. They use lures to get them to run. Some have higher prey drives than others. Tucker has a low enough drive that he's considered cat safe."

"Cat safe?" She narrowed her eyes at him. "You're sure?"

"He'll probably just ignore the cat." He stood there waiting for her to open the door, but she wasn't convinced yet.

"Will he chew on my shoes?" she asked.

"He's not a chewer. He's a collector."

"What, like stamps?"

Nick grinned. "Cell phones, remote controls, sometimes car keys, but his favorite is slippers. The smellier the better. He's also been known to take the salt and pepper shakers off the table. If anything is missing, his bed is the first place I look."

She looked down at the dog. He looked back up

at her with forlorn brown eyes that begged, "Please love me."

"He won't pee on my rug?"

"He's housebroken. He also doesn't bark, barely sheds and he sleeps twenty-three hours of the day. He's not going to be a problem. In fact, he'll love having a fenced yard to run around."

She looked at the dog, then back at Nick.

"Are you going to let us in? I'm on excessive doses of allergy medication so I can be around your cat. You can at least give Tucker a chance."

He was right. How much trouble could one over-sized dog be?

Scratch that. She probably didn't want to know.

She unlocked the door and opened it. "Sorry about the mess. I didn't have time to clean."

Nick and Tucker stepped inside and the room suddenly felt an awful lot smaller. He unsnapped the leash and hung it on the coat tree and Tucker, being a dog, went straight for Zoë's crotch. He gave her a sniff, then looked up, as if he were expecting something. He was even bigger than he looked standing on the porch.

"He's enormous."

"He's an extra large." Nick shrugged out of his leather jacket and hung it over the leash.

"Why is he staring at me?"

"He wants you to pet him."

"Oh." She patted the top of his head gingerly. "Nice doggie."

Satisfied that he'd been adequately welcomed, Tucker trotted off to explore, his nails click-clicking on the hardwood floor. "Will he be okay by himself?"

"Yeah, he won't get into anything."

She gestured to Nick's lone bag. "Is that all you brought?"

"I have a few more things in the truck. I figure as I need stuff I can run over to my place and pick it up."

"I'm giving you the spare bedroom," she told him.

He flashed her a curious look. "I don't remember agreeing to that."

"I think at this point sex will only complicate things." He'd proven that this afternoon when he had kissed her. Her brain had been so overdrenched in pheromones she would have agreed to practically anything. "We should ease into this slowly. We need to get used to living together. We need to be sure this relationship isn't just physical."

That sexy grin curled his mouth. The guy was un-believably smug. "You really think you can resist me?"

She hoped so, but she could see by the devious glint in his eye he wasn't going to make it easy. "I'll manage."

From the kitchen Zoë heard a hiss, then an ear-splitting canine yip, and Tucker darted into the living room, skidding clumsily across the floor, long gangly legs flailing. Whining like a big baby, he scurried over to Nick and hid behind him. In the kitchen doorway sat Dexter, all whopping eight pounds of him, casually licking one fluffy white paw as though he didn't have a care in the world.

So much for the dog ignoring the cat.

"He's bleeding," Nick said indignantly, examining Tucker's nose. "Your cat attacked my dog."

"I'm sure he was provoked." She found herself feeling very proud of Dexter for protecting his domain. No big dopey dog was going to push him around. "They probably just need time to get used to each other."

Kind of like her and Nick.

"So," she said, suddenly feeling awkward. "I guess we should get you settled in."

Nick followed her down the hall to one of the two downstairs bedrooms. On the left was her office, and on the right her guest room. He stepped inside, taking in the frilly curtains and lacey spread.

"Pink?" He cringed, as though it was painful to look at. "I can feel my testosterone drying up. Maybe I should just sleep on the couch. Or in a tent in the backyard."

"Don't be such a baby," she said and he tossed his bag on the bed. "I was thinking we could just get carryout for dinner."

He shrugged. "Works for me."

"We can order, and while we're waiting for it to be delivered, we can get the rest of your things out of the truck."

He followed her to the kitchen and she pulled open her junk drawer. It held a menu from every local restaurant within delivering distance. "What are you in the mood for," she asked, and he gave her that simmering, sexy look, so she added, "besides *that*."

He grinned. "I'm not picky. You're the pregnant one. You choose."

She chose pizza. A staple item for her these days. The cheesier and gooier the better.

While they waited for it, they brought in the last of his things, most of which were for the dog who lay snoozing on his bed in the living room, occasionally opening one eye to peek around. Probably to make sure the cat was a safe distance away. Dexter lounged on the front windowsill pretending not to notice him.

It wasn't as if Nick had never been to her house, but showing him around, inviting him into her private domain, was just too weird. He would be using her towels to dry himself, washing his clothes in her washing machine and eating food from her dishes. It was so intimate and invasive. The enormity of it all hadn't really hit her until she'd seen him on the porch. She hadn't realized just how used to living alone she'd become in the past ten years. Most of the single women she knew who were her age or younger were looking for a companion. They wanted Mr. Right. She only wanted Mr. Right Now.

Not that she wasn't going to try to make this work.

The tour ended in the kitchen, and when Nick opened the fridge, he frowned. It was pitifully empty. But the freezer was stuffed wall-to-wall with Lean Cuisine dinners.

He gave her a look, and she shrugged. "There was a good sale so I stocked up."

"There's no real food in here," he said. "Don't you *ever* cook?"

Never. It was one of the few things her mother hadn't made her do. She had this nasty habit of burning things. The last time she attempted to cook herself a real meal, she'd wandered out of the room without shutting off the heat under a greasy frying pan and had set her kitchen on fire. Thank God she had a smoke detector and a good fire extinguisher. "Trust me when I say, we're both a lot safer if I don't cook."

For a second she thought he might ask for an explanation, then he just shook his head. He probably figured he was better off not knowing.

"Besides, who needs real food when you have carryout and prenatal vitamins?" she asked cheerfully.

He began opening cupboards, one by one, taking inventory of their lack of contents, shaking his head. Did he think the real food was going to miraculously appear?

"What are you doing?" she asked.

"Making a mental list so I know what to buy. Which at this point is pretty much everything."

"You can buy all the food you want, as long as you don't expect me to cook it."

"It may surprise you to learn that I'm not half bad when it comes to preparing a meal. It's one of the few things I remember doing with my mom."

Though he tried to hide it, she could see a dash of

wistful sadness flash across his face. The way it always did when he mentioned his mom.

"How old were you?"

"Five or six I guess."

"She was okay then?"

He shrugged. "I don't know if you could ever say she was completely okay. But life would be almost normal for months at a time, then the meds would stop working, or the side effects would be so bad she would stop taking them. Gradually she got so bad, nothing seemed to work. I was eight when social services removed me."

"And you haven't seen her since?"

He shook his head. "Nope."

She couldn't imagine going all those years without seeing her parents. Not knowing where they were or what they were doing.

"I used to get an occasional letter, but not for about six years now. She moved around a lot, going from shelter to shelter. I haven't been able to find her."

"What would you do if you did find her?"

"I'd try to get her in an institution or a group home. Her mental illness is degenerative. She won't ever get better, or even be able to function in society. But the truth is, she's probably dead by now."

He sounded almost cold. If she hadn't known Nick so well, she might have missed the hint of sadness in his tone. It made her want to pull him in her arms and give him a big hug. How could he stand it, not knowing if she was dead or alive? Not knowing if she was out there somewhere suffering. Cold and lonely and hungry.

"Are you worried about the baby?" he asked.

"What do you mean?"

"About the fact that mental illness can be genetic."

Honestly, she'd never even considered that. She didn't know all that much about mental illness, and even less about genetics. "Should I be worried?"

"My mom's illness stems from brain damage she sustained in a car wreck when she was a kid. So no, the baby won't be predisposed to it. Unless it runs on your side."

"My parents had nine kids, which if you ask me is completely nuts. But as far as I know, neither of them are technically mentally ill. Unless it was some big secret, I don't recall *anyone* in my family ever being mentally ill. And it's a big family."

"Speaking of big families, that's something we've never talked about," he said. "If this does work out, and we decide to get married, how will you feel about having more kids?"

Did the phrase, *over my dead body* mean anything to him? And how would he react if she was adamant about not having any more children.

That was something they would worry about later, when it became clear how far they planned to take this.

"I'm not sure," she told him, which wasn't completely untrue. There was a chance, however slim, that she would agree on one more baby.

"It's something I feel strongly about," he added.

She could see that, and she couldn't help feeling they were starting with one strike already against them.

Five

Zoë woke at eleven-thirty Saturday morning with a painfully full bladder and a warm weight resting on her feet. She pried her lids open and looked to the foot of the bed to find a pair of hopeful brown eyes gazing back at her.

"What are you doing in my bed?" Just her luck, Tucker was one of those dogs attracted to humans who didn't like them. She gave him a nudge with her foot. "Shoo. Get lost."

Tucker exhaled a long-suffering sigh and dropped his head down on the comforter, eyes sad. Up on the dresser beside the bed, Dexter watched over them, giving Tucker the evil eye.

"Go sleep in your own bed." She gave him another

gentle shove. He tried one more forlorn look, and she pointed to the door. "Out."

With a sigh he unfolded his lanky body and jumped down from the bed, landing with a thud on the rug, the tags on his collar jingling as he trotted out the door and down the stairs.

She sat up and her stomach did a quick pitch and roll. So far she'd gotten away with negligible morning sickness. A bit of queasiness first thing in the morning that usually settled after she choked down a bagel or muffin.

She eased herself out of bed and shoved her arms into her robe, but when she looked down for her slippers they were no longer on the side of the bed where she was sure she'd left them.

Darn dog.

She shuffled half-asleep across the ice-cold bare floor and down the stairs to the bathroom. She smelled something that resembled food and her stomach gave an empty moan followed by a slightly questionable grumble. She used the facilities and brushed her teeth. She tried to brush her hair into submission and wound up with a head full of blond frizz.

Oh well. If he was going to stay here, he would have to learn to live with the fact that she woke up looking like a beast. It also hadn't escaped her attention that the bathroom smelled decidedly more male than it had the previous morning, and when she opened the medicine chest, she found a shelf full of *guy* things there. Aftershave, cologne, shaving gel and a razor. Along with several other tubes and bottles of various male things.

She shook her head. Weird.

She found her way to the kitchen, doing a double take as she passed through the living room. She blinked and rubbed her eyes, sure that it was an illusion. But no, the clutter was gone. The newspapers and old magazines and dirty dishes. The random tufts of cat fluff had been vacuumed away. He'd even dusted.

A man who did housework? Had she died and gone to heaven, or had she woken up in the twilight zone?

Tucker lay on his bed beside the couch, the tips of two furry pink slippers sticking out from under his belly. *Her* slippers.

"Give my slippers back you mangy thief." Tucker just gazed back at her with innocent brown eyes that said, *Slippers? What slippers?*

Since he didn't seem inclined to move any time soon, she reached down and tugged them out from under him. Lucky for the dog they weren't chewed up and covered with slobber. Regardless, she would have to start keeping them on the top shelf of her closet.

She found Nick in the kitchen standing at the stove, cooking something that looked like an omelet. He wore a red flannel shirt with the sleeves rolled to his elbows, one that accentuated the wide breadth of his shoulders. His perfect behind was tucked into a pair of faded blue jeans that weren't quite tight, but not exactly loose either. On his feet he wore steel-toed leather work boots.

"That smells good."

Nick turned and smiled. "'Morning."

He was showered and shaved and way too cheerful. He looked her up and down and asked, "Rough night?"

"You know those women who wake up looking well-rested and radiant? I'm not one of them."

He only grinned. He probably figured silence was his best defense. To say she didn't look like a troll would be a lie, and to admit it would hurt her feelings.

Smart man.

"Thanks for cleaning up," she said. "You didn't have to do that."

"If I'm going to live here, I'm going to pitch in." He turned back to the stove. "The eggs will be done in a minute and there's juice in the fridge."

Juice?

She had no juice. Just a half gallon of skim milk that went chunky three days ago. Come to think of it, she didn't have eggs, either. Or the bacon that was frying in the skillet beside the nonexistent eggs. Or the hash brown patties sitting in the toaster. "Where did all this food come from?"

"I went shopping."

He shopped, too? She *was* in the twilight zone.

"If you're trying to impress me, it's working." She opened the refrigerator and found it packed with food. Milk, juice and eggs and bags of fresh fruit and vegetables. She wondered if he did windows, too. "What else have you done this morning?"

He grabbed two plates from the cupboard. It sure hadn't taken him long to familiarize himself with her kitchen. "I jogged, showered, cleaned and shopped, and I stopped by my place to pick up a few more things."

"Jeez, when did you get up?"

"Fiveish."

"It's Saturday."

He shrugged. "What can I say—I'm a morning person."

"I'm sorry, but that is just sick and wrong." Not that it wasn't kind of nice waking up and having breakfast ready. She poured herself a glass of organic apple juice—organic?—and sat at the table in the nook. Nick set a plate of food in front of her. Eggs, bacon, hash browns and buttered toast. She wondered if it was real butter. "Looks good. Thanks."

Nick slid into the seat across from her, dwarfing the small table, his booted feet bumping her toes. Invading her space. The man took up so much darned room.

She closed her eyes and said a short, silent, guilt induced blessing. A holdover from her strict Catholic upbringing. Some traditions were just impossible to break.

Nick dug right into his breakfast and, like everything else, ate with enthusiasm and gusto. No doubt about it, the guy enjoyed life to the fullest.

She picked at her food, nibbling tiny bites and chasing it down with sips of juice.

"Not hungry?" he asked.

"Not really." She bit off a wedge of toast. "Mild morning sickness."

"Anything I can do?"

"You could have the baby for me."

He gave her a "yeah, you wish" look.

After a few minutes of nibbling, her stomach gradually began to settle, and she began to feel her appetite returning. Though she didn't typically eat a big breakfast, she stopped just short of picking up her plate and licking it clean. She even reached across the table to nab the last slice of bacon off Nick's plate.

"Not hungry, huh?"

"I guess I was hungrier than I thought."

Nick got up and cleared the dishes from the table. "I was thinking about heading into the office for a few hours. Want to tag along?"

She had enough of the office Monday through Friday. Her weekends were hers. "I don't think so."

Normally she would wait until after dinner to do the day's dishes—sometimes three days later—but out of guilt she took the dirty plates and juice glasses from the sink and stacked them in the dishwasher. "It's supposed to get up in the high fifties today. I was planning on working in the garden. I need to get my gladiola bulbs planted."

"Then I'll stay and help."

She closed the dishwasher and wiped her hands on a towel. "Nick, your living here doesn't mean we'll be attached at the hip. We don't have to spend every second of the day together."

"I'm not asking for every second of your time. But I'm also not looking for a roommate I'll only see in passing." He folded a work-roughened hand over her shoulder. Its warm weight began to do funny things to her insides. "If we're going to do this, we're going to do it right. We're going to be a couple."

A couple of *what*, that was the question.

A couple of idiots for thinking this might actually work? Or a couple of fools for not realizing they were too different for this kind of relationship?

Having a big, strapping man around definitely had its advantages.

It might have taken Zoë two or three weekends to turn over the dirt to create a new flower garden and prepare it for planting. That meant two or three weeks of sore arms, an aching back and dirty fingernails. Nick, macho guy that he was, had nearly the entire area turned over and de-sodded in three hours.

She'd offered to help, but he said he would never let a woman in her condition do a man's job. Normally a comment like that would have gotten him a whack over the head with a shovel, but then he started driving the pitchfork into the soil and she became distracted watching the powerful flex of his thighs against worn denim. The way they cupped his behind just right.

As the temperature climbed up close to sixty, Nick shed first his jacket, then he peeled off his tattered Yale sweatshirt. She found herself increasingly distracted from her chore of picking weeds from the turned soil and dumping them in a bucket to go in the compost pile. She was much more interested in watching the play of muscles under the thin, white, sweat-soaked T-shirt.

What would it feel like to touch him again? What would he do if she got up right now and ran her hand up his back…

She shook away the thought. No. *Bad Zoë.* No touching allowed. Not yet anyway. Not until it was clear this relationship wasn't based solely on sex.

He was just so…*male.* And she was suffering from a serious excess of estrogen or pheromones, or whichever hormone it was that made a woman feel like molesting every man in sight.

One would never guess from the look of him that Nick had been raised among the rich and sophisticated. Not that he gave the impression of being a thug, either. He wore jeans and a flannel shirt the way most other men wore a three piece suit. When Nick entered a room, no matter the size, he filled it. He drew attention with his strength and character. With his unwavering confidence and larger-than-life presence. But he was so easygoing, he could impress without intimidating.

He was also a loyal friend and a fair employer. The kind of man a person could count on.

That didn't mean he was a pushover, though. People didn't mess with Nick. He may have had the patience of a saint, but cross him and watch out. His wick was long, but the impending explosion was catastrophic.

Something bumped Zoë's shoulder and she turned

from watching Nick to find a long snout in her face. Before she could react, Tucker gave her a big sloppy kiss right on the mouth.

"Aaaagh!" She frantically wiped dog slobber off her face with the sleeve of her sweater. "Go away, you disgusting animal!"

Nick turned to see what the problem was. "What's wrong?"

"Your dog just slobbered on my face."

Nick grinned. He probably trained the dog to do that just to annoy her. "That's his way of saying he likes you."

"Couldn't he find a less disgusting way to show affection? One that doesn't involve his spit."

He drove the pitchfork into the ground and leaned on the handle, a bead of sweat running down the side of his face. "I've been thinking about this arrangement we have and it occurred to me that we've been out together lots of times, but never as a couple."

"Like a date?"

"Right. So I was wondering if maybe you would like to go out with me tonight."

"As a couple?"

"I was thinking something along the lines of dinner and a movie."

Interesting. "Like a *real* date?"

"Yep."

She hadn't been on *any* kind of date—real or pretend—in longer that she wanted to admit. Her social life had been less than exciting lately. Most men seemed to want one thing, and they expected it on the first date no less. She obviously had no objections to sex before marriage, but even she thought two people should get to know each other before they hopped in the sack together.

"I get pregnant, you move in, *then* you ask me out on a date. Amazing how backward we're doing all of this, isn't it?"

"Is that a yes?"

"Yes. I'd love to go on a date with you."

He surveyed the ground he had yet to turn over. "This should only take me another fifteen or twenty minutes. Then I'll need to shower."

"Me, too. Why don't I hop in first while you finish up."

She hiked herself up, brushing dirt from her gardening gloves and the knees of her jeans. She knew it was something she would have to get used to, but the idea of showering while he was in her house was a little weird. Maybe if she hurried, she could get in and out while he was still outside.

Unless he wanted to conserve water and shower together…

No. *Bad* Zoë.

She gave herself a mental slap. There would be no shower sharing. At least not yet. But that *was* something couples did, right?

"One more thing," Nick called after her as she dashed to the house. She turned and found him flashing her that simmering, sexy smile.

Uh-oh, what was he up to?

"Since this is a real date, I'll be expecting a good-night kiss."

Nick glanced through the darkness at Zoë. She sat beside him in the truck, her head resting against the window, a damp tissue crumpled in her hand. Since they left the theater, her sobs had calmed to an occasional hiccup and sniffle.

On a first date disaster scale of one to ten, they had ranked a solid eleven. But technically the date wouldn't be over until they got home, so he wasn't going to count his chickens. It could get a lot better—or a lot worse.

Agreeing on a movie had been the first hitch. She had wanted to go to some artsy foreign film playing in Birmingham, and he wanted to see the latest martial arts action flick.

After a long debate-argument, they finally compromised—he being the one to do most of the compromising—and agreed on a romantic comedy.

As a trade-off, she'd let him pick the restaurant this time. He chose a four-star Middle Eastern place in Southfield he'd heard fantastic things about. He'd also learned a valuable lesson. Never try to feed a pregnant woman new, exotic food. When the server had set their plates in front of them, the unfamiliar textures and scents had turned her skin a peculiar shade of green. One bite had her bolting to the bathroom.

She'd had to wait outside while he paid the bill and the waitress packed up their uneaten dinner in carryout containers.

Since they were both still hungry, they had stopped at a fast food drive-thru and ate burgers and fries on the way to the theater.

He didn't normally get into chick flicks, but the film hadn't been as boring as he had anticipated, and their experience at the movie theater had been blessedly uneventful. Until the end, that is, when Zoë dissolved into uncontrollable sobs. Which was a little strange considering the movie had a happy ending. She'd been crying so hard he'd practically had to carry her out of the theater.

He'd gotten more than a few evil looks from female moviegoers—as if her emotional breakdown was somehow his fault—and several sympathetic head shakes from their male counterparts.

He wasn't going to pretend he had even the slightest clue what had happened. Or how to fix it. What he did know was that good night kiss he was hoping for seemed unlikely at this point. As did any possibility of seducing his way into her bed.

Beside him, Zoë sniffed and dabbed at her eyes with a tissue.

"You okay?" he asked, giving her shoulder a reassuring pat.

She wiped her nose and said in a wobbly voice, "I ruined our first date."

Ruined was such a strong word. There had been

good points. Given time, he could probably think up a few. "You didn't ruin anything."

"I got sick at dinner then had a breakdown in the movie theater."

He was going to say that it could have been worse, but they were still a few minutes from home. No point tempting fate.

"What if it's a sign?" she hiccupped. "What if this is God's way of telling us our relationship is going to be a disaster? Maybe this is our punishment for the premarital sex."

He'd never spent much time with a pregnant woman, but he was almost one hundred percent sure this was one of those mood swings he'd heard expectant fathers talk about. "Zoë, I think this has more to do with hormones than divine intervention."

"It was our first date. It was supposed to be special."

It was completely off the wall, but despite the fact that her face was all swollen and blotchy and her nose was running, he didn't think he'd ever seen her look more beautiful.

It wasn't often he got the opportunity to take care of Zoë. She was so damned capable and independent. He liked that she needed him. That she had a vulnerable side.

He took her free hand, linking his fingers through hers. "Just being with you made it special."

She looked up at him through the dark, tears welling in her red, puffy eyes and leaking down her cheeks. "That's s-so s-sweet."

But not so sweet that she would be willing to spend the rest of her life with him.

The words sat on the tip of his tongue but he bit them back. He had no interest in trying to guilt her into marriage. If and when they exchanged vows, he wanted her to mean every word she said.

And if that never happened? If she decided she didn't want to marry him?

Well, they would burn that bridge when they came to it.

Six

Sunday—thank goodness—proved to be a quiet and uneventful day. Zoë woke once again to a hot breakfast, and after the kitchen was cleaned, she and Nick had lounged around, chatting and reading the newspaper. Nick had adopted the recliner and Zoë shared the couch with the dog—who in two days had become her shadow. Later Nick watched football and drank beer while she retaught herself to knit, in the hopes of making the baby a blanket.

It felt so…domestic. And though she had never been a big fan of football—or any sport for that matter—it was nice just being in the same room with him, each doing their own thing. It had been…comfortable.

Isn't that how her parents had done it? When they

weren't working that is, which wasn't very often. Her father would park himself in the La-Z-Boy and her mom would grade papers or do needlepoint.

Maybe that was what all real couples did.

Nick fixed authentic, spicy enchiladas for dinner, which as he promised were delicious. And were probably the reason she woke Monday morning feeling as if someone had siphoned battery acid into her stomach.

She didn't manage to drag herself to work until after ten. She knew there was a problem the instant she stepped into her office and saw Shannon sitting at her desk, a determined look on her face.

The kiss.

She'd been so wrapped up in the living together thing, she had completely forgotten someone saw her and Nick kissing on Friday. Obviously, it had gotten around and Shannon was expecting an explanation.

Zoë shrugged out of her jacket and collapsed into her visitor's chair, since her own chair was occupied. "Go ahead, get it over with."

"It isn't bad enough that you don't tell me you're playing hide the salami with the boss—"

"Charming," Zoë interjected.

"—but this morning I take a call from your doctor's office and I'm told your prescription has been called into the pharmacy. Your prescription for *prenatal vitamins.*"

Oh crud. Zoë felt all the blood drain from her face.

Shannon smiled smugly. "Is there by any chance something you neglected to tell me?"

Zoë winced. The kiss getting out was bad enough. She really wasn't ready for everyone to find out about her pregnancy.

"I admit I was deeply hurt."

She didn't look hurt. She looked as if she was preparing to give Zoë a thorough razzing. That was definitely more her style. Zoë and everyone else in the office had learned not to take it personally. Shannon leaned forward, elbows on the desk, fingers steepled under her chin. "But considering you probably just made me five-hundred and thirty-eight dollars richer, I might have to forgive you."

Five-hundred and thirty-eight dollars? "How did I manage that?"

"I won the pool."

"*Pool?*" Why did she get the feeling she didn't want to know what Shannon was talking about?

"Every time Nick skips out on a fiancée there's a betting pool to guess how long it will take him to find a replacement. I said within a week."

"The office has been *betting* on Nick's dating habits?" How is it that she had never heard about this?

"There's been some obvious tension between you guys since the wedding. Lots of long lingering looks when the other isn't watching. I put two and two together." She flashed Zoë a smug smile. "Looks like I was right, huh?"

She so did not need this hassle. There would be

questions that required explanations she just wasn't ready to give.

Zoë blew out a breath. "Who knows?"

"About you and Nick sucking face? Pretty much the whole office. It was Tiffany that walked in on you."

"I should have known, she never knocks." She also had a big mouth, and Zoë was pretty sure she had a crush on Nick.

"What about the baby? How many people know about that?"

Shannon sat back in the chair. "You see, that's tricky. Without telling everyone, I'll have a hard time proving the entire timeline, and the fact that I actually won. I had to ask myself, what's more important to me? Our friendship or being able to buy that forty inch flat screen television I've had my eye on. And as a result, reap the reward of many weeks of fantastic sex from my very grateful spouse."

"So it all boils down to our friendship or good sex?"

"You may not believe this, but after three kids and ten years of marriage, good sex can be pretty hard to come by."

Which probably meant that her secret didn't have a chance of hell in staying that way. "So what did you decide?"

She grinned. "That our friendship means more to me. But, honey, you're going to owe me big time for this one."

"Thank-you," Zoë said softly, close to tears again. Which was so not her. She never cried.

Would this emotional roller-coaster ride never end?

"That doesn't mean I don't want details. So spill."

"We didn't plan this," she told Shannon. "It was supposed to be a one time thing. A drunken mistake."

"But you got a little surprise instead?"

Zoë nodded. "The whole thing is a fluke."

"This was no fluke, Zoë."

She wished she could believe that. "He asked me to marry him."

Shannon didn't look surprised. "That sounds about right for Nick. What did you tell him?"

"That I'm not ready for that. We've decided to try living together for a while first."

"Which sounds about right for you."

Zoë frowned. "What's that supposed to mean?"

"No offense, but you *always* play it safe. You keep everyone at arm's length."

"I do not!" Zoë said, feeling instantly defensive. "You and I have been friends for a long time."

"And you know pretty much everything about me, right?"

"I guess so."

"And what do I know about you? What have you told me about your family?"

She bit her lip, trying to remember what she might have told Shannon, a sinking feeling in her chest. "You, um, know I have a big family."

"I know there are nine of you, but I have no idea how many brothers or sisters you have. I don't know their names. I know you grew up in Petoskey but you never talk about what it was like there. How it was for you growing up. You never talk about school or friends. *Nothing* personal. To get you to open up at all I have to practically drag it out of you. You have a lot of friends here, but besides Nick, I don't think *anyone* really knows you."

She hated to admit it, but Shannon was right. Zoë didn't get personal with too many people. Just her sister and Nick, and Nick hadn't been by choice. He had just sort of insinuated himself into her life, settling in like a pesky houseguest who never left. And there had always been a bit of resistance on her part. There still was. She always held a tiny piece of herself back.

Was Shannon right? Had Zoë been keeping everyone at arm's length?

An uneasy feeling settled in her stomach. Maybe her aversion to marriage had less to do with her family and was instead just a strange quirk in her personality. Maybe she'd never learned how to let herself open up to people. And if she didn't change, what kind of future could she and Nick possibly have? If they had one at all. If she refused to marry him, would it ruin their friendship? Would they wind up resenting each other?

The thought made her heart shudder with fear.

Nick was such a huge part of her life. What would she do without him?

If they were going to make this work, she would have to learn to open up and let him in.

All the way in.

"I'm not saying this to hurt your feelings," Shannon said, looking apologetic. "I think you're a wonderful, kind person. I consider you a good friend. Which is why I'd like to see this thing with Nick work out. You may not realize it now, but you two are perfect for each other."

"I told him no sex," Zoë blurted out, then turned twenty different shades of red. Why had she said that?

Shannon's eyes rounded. "No sex? Ever?"

"Not ever. Just until we're sure our relationship isn't just physical."

"One night of sex in what, ten years of friendship, and you're worried the relationship is only physical?"

Zoë hadn't realized until just now how ridiculous that sounded. And how equally ridiculous it must have sounded to Nick. What he must think of her.

"Do you think denying him sex is my way of keeping him at arm's length?"

"Honey, it doesn't matter what I think. The question is, what do *you* think?"

She was thinking that insisting they live together first had been her roundabout way of putting off making a difficult decision. One that shouldn't have been difficult in the first place. After ten years of friendship, she should know what she was feeling. Either she loved him or she didn't.

And if she didn't, maybe it was only because she hadn't let herself.

Nick had been incredibly patient with her so far, but

at some point he was going to grow tired of chasing her. How could she risk losing the one man she might have been destined to spend the rest of her life with?

She had to make a decision, and she had to make it soon.

"I don't care what his excuse is," Nick barked into the phone. His foreman, John Miglione, had just delivered the news that one of his employees had left for lunch and failed to return—for the fourth time in two weeks. On top of that the man called in sick at least once a week. There was nothing Nick hated more than firing people, but he needed reliable employees. A smart man knew that to survive in business he should surround himself with competent people. The weak links had to go. "Tell him one more time and he's out of a job."

"Will do, Nick. And there's one more thing."

He was silent for a second, as if he were working up to something, and Nick knew exactly what that something was.

"I know you want to ask, so just go ahead and get it over with."

"Is it true about you and Zoë?"

"That depends on what you heard."

"That Tiffany walked in on you two getting down and dirty."

"Tiffany exaggerates. It was just a kiss."

"Does that mean you two are…"

"Possibly. We're giving it a trial run."

"Well, it's about time."

Nick shook his head. "Do you know that you're the third person who said that to me today."

Zoë appeared in his office doorway—speak of the devil. He held up a finger to let her know he would only be a minute.

John laughed. "Then that should tell you something, genius. Give her a big wet one for me. I'll talk to you later."

He shook his head and hung up the phone, turning to Zoë. "What's up?"

"Is this a bad time?" she asked.

"No. John just called about O'Connell. He didn't come back after lunch—again. He seemed like a decent guy when we hired him. Overqualified even, but he can't seem to get his act together."

"That's too bad." She closed and locked the office door.

Did they have a meeting he'd forgotten? And if so, why lock the door?

Without a word she crossed the room and walked around his desk looking very...*determined*.

Determined to do what, he wasn't sure.

There was definitely something up.

"What's going on?" he asked.

With her eyes pinned on his face, she began unbuttoning her blouse.

Huh?

He watched as she slipped the garment off her shoulders and let it drop to the floor. He was too stunned to do anything but sit there as she climbed in his lap. She straddled his legs, her skirt bunching at her upper thighs, wrapped her arms around his neck and kissed him.

No, this wasn't just a kiss. This was a sexual attack. A wet, deep, oral assault. And he was completely defenseless.

He knew she was passionate, but man, he'd never expected this.

She feasted on his mouth, clawing her fingers through his hair, arching her body against him. She rode him like he was her own personal amusement park attraction.

It was hot as hell, the way she was throwing herself at him, still, something wasn't right. Something he couldn't quite put his finger on.

Something was…*missing*.

He felt her tugging his shirt from the waist of his jeans, fumbling with the buckle on his belt.

What the heck was going on?

He wasn't one to turn down sex, even if it was in the middle of the afternoon in his office. In fact, the idea of sex *anywhere* with Zoë was enough to get his engine primed, but something about this just wasn't right. She was kissing him, rubbing her satin and lace-covered breasts against his chest, yet he wasn't feeling a damn thing. He didn't even have a hard-on.

He grabbed Zoë's shoulders, held her at arm's length and asked, "What are you doing?"

"Seducing you," she said, like that should have

been completely obvious, sounding more exasperated than turned on.

"I see that. But why?"

She looked at him as though he was speaking an alien language. "Why?"

"You said you wanted to wait," he reminded her.

"I'm not allowed to change my mind?"

"Of course you are." But he had a strong feeling she hadn't changed her mind, or something had changed it without her consent. It was as if she was going through the motions, but her heart wasn't really in it. "Just tell me why."

She blew out an exasperated breath. "Do I need a reason? Jeez! I thought you would be jumping at the chance. I thought you would have me naked by now."

"Normally, I would. It just feels like…I don't know. Like you're doing this because you have to. Or I'm forcing you or something."

"You're *not* forcing me."

"I'm sorry, but something about this just doesn't feel right."

A delicate little wrinkle formed between her brows. "Are you turning me down?"

It was hard for him to believe, too. In fact, he couldn't think of a single time when he'd turned a woman down. "At least until you tell me what's up. Why the sudden change of heart?"

She slid out of his lap, snatched her shirt up from the floor and covered herself with it. "I thought this was what you wanted."

He could see that he'd hurt her feelings, but he needed to know what was going on. They had to be honest with each other or this relationship would never have a chance.

"Of course it's what I want. But is it what you want?"

She gave him that confused look again. "I don't understand. I'm here, aren't I?"

"Zoë, why did you come in here?"

She tugged her shirt on and buttoned it. "You know why."

"What I mean is, what *motivated* you?"

Her frown deepened. "I wanted to have sex with you."

He sighed. This was going nowhere. "Let's try this. Let me give you a scenario, and you tell me if I'm right. Okay?"

She nodded and smoothed the creases from her wrinkled skirt.

"You were sitting at your desk thinking about me, remembering that night in the hotel. You became so overcome with lust and passion that you couldn't wait another minute to have me, so you raced down to my office."

She just stared at him, so he asked, "Was it something like that?"

She bit her lip. "Um…"

He was a little disappointed, but not surprised. "Talk to me Zoë. Tell me what's going on."

"I thought that if I didn't have sex with you soon, maybe you were going to get sick of waiting.

Maybe you would find someone else. Someone… better."

That had to be the dumbest thing he had ever heard. "Contrary to what you might believe, a man can go three days living with a woman and not have sex." He leaned back in the chair and folded his arms over his chest. "Hell, there have been times I've lasted a whole week. And if it becomes a problem, there's no reason why I can't…take matters into my own hands, so to speak."

Her cheeks flushed pink and she lowered her eyes to the floor. It amazed him that a woman who so excelled at talking dirty could possibly be embarrassed by this conversation.

He patted his legs. "Come'ere. Have a seat."

She hesitated—the woman who had just thrown herself at him with guns blazing—then sat primly on his knee, tucking her skirt around her legs.

This was definitely not going to cut it.

He wrapped his hands around her waist. She gasped as he pulled her snug against his chest, her behind tucked firmly into his lap.

That was much better.

"Okay, now what made you think I would dump you if you didn't sleep with me?"

She looked up at him, so much conflict and confusion in her eyes. "I keep everyone at arm's length."

"Arm's length?" What was she talking about?

"I'm too private. I don't let people in. You're

going to get sick of me shutting you out and find someone else."

Where was she getting this garbage? How could a woman so intelligent act so dumb? "And sex is supposed to fix that?"

She shrugged. "It's a start."

"Do you honestly think I'm that shallow?"

She shook her head, looking guilty for even thinking it.

"If I thought you were shutting me out emotionally, sex ten times a day wouldn't make a damned bit of difference."

She gnawed at the skin on her lower lip. "I guess I never thought of it like that."

"I guess not." He brushed a few wayward blond curls back and tucked them behind her ear. "You must have had a good reason for wanting to wait, and I respect that. If you're not ready, that's okay. I understand."

The crinkle in her brow grew deeper. "That's just it. I'm not sure if the reason I had was a good one. We've been friends for years and managed not to have sex. So why would I think our relationship would only be physical? And it's not like I don't want to have sex. It's all I think about lately. When I'm not sick, or sobbing my eyes out, that is."

A grin curled his mouth.

"I have this really annoying habit of looking at your butt. I never even used to notice it, and now I can't peel my eyes off of it. And I want to touch it. I want to touch you *everywhere*. So why am I still telling you no?"

He shrugged. She was adorable when she was confused and frustrated.

"I'm afraid I'm doing it because I don't let people close to me."

"Maybe it's just that you're dealing with an awful lot right now and a sexual relationship is more than you're ready for."

"You think?" she asked, a hopeful look in her eyes.

"When I make love to you, Zoë, I want it to be like that night in the hotel. I want you to want me as much as I want you."

Her lips curved in a dreamy smile. "It really was good, wasn't it?"

He couldn't help grinning himself. "Oh, yeah."

She cupped his face in her hands. Her skin was warm and soft and smelled like soap. "You know what? You're a great guy."

Then she kissed him. A sweet, tender kiss packed with so much simple, genuine affection it nearly knocked him out of his chair.

Now, this was definitely more like it. He would rather hold and kiss her this way for five minutes than have an entire night of meaningless sex.

That night in the hotel he knew that there was something more between them. Something they had both buried away. Maybe she just wasn't ready to take that last step. But she would be eventually.

He was certain of it.

Seven

When Zoë pulled into her driveway later that evening there was a car parked there.

"Oh, fudge."

That's what she got for dodging her sister's calls. And giving her a key. She should have known that if she didn't come clean, Faith would pop in for a surprise visit.

Maybe she subconsciously wanted her here. Maybe she needed someone to tell her what to do.

She parked her conservative Volvo beside her sister's flashy little crimson Miata. They had always been polar opposites. Zoë the practical, responsible sister and Faith the wild child.

When they were kids, Faith had always wanted to

loosen Zoë up and teach her to have fun, while Zoë ran herself ragged trying to keep Faith out of trouble. If their parents knew how many times Zoë had covered for her when she'd snuck out after midnight to meet a boyfriend or go to a wild party, they would have strokes.

She gathered her things and headed for the front door. She stepped inside and called, "I'm home."

Faith appeared from the kitchen, her flame-red hair cut stylishly short and gelled into spiky points, a drastic change from the waist-length curls she'd had last time. She was dressed in body-hugging black jeans and a stretchy chenille sweater the exact same green as her eyes.

She clicked across the room in spiked high heels and hugged Zoë fiercely. "Surprise!"

"What are you doing here?" she asked, wrapped up in a scented cloud of perfume and hairspray.

"Don't even pretend you don't know why I'm here. You haven't been returning my calls and that always means something is wrong."

"Nothing is wrong, I promise." She stepped back and looked her sister up and down. She looked perfect, as usual. She wore just enough makeup to look attractive, without being overdone. Her acrylic nails were just the right length and painted a warm shade of pink. Attractive, but not overly flashy. Faith has always been the pretty one. "You look gorgeous! I love the new haircut."

"And you look exhausted. But don't even change the

subject. Why was there an enormous dog in your house and what's with all the guy stuff in the spare bedroom?"

"Those are Nick's things. So is the dog." She looked around, wondering why Tucker hadn't met her at the door. She was kind of getting used to the crotch sniff greetings and sloppy dog kisses. "Where is the dog?"

"I let him out. And why is Nick staying here? Is he getting his place sprayed for bugs or something?"

Before Zoë could explain, the front door opened and Nick walked though, his regular old big gorgeous self. She saw him through different eyes now and couldn't help wondering if it would be obvious to the world what she was feeling. Not that she thought there was a snowball's chance in hell of keeping this from her sister now.

"Pork chop!" Nick said, giving Faith a big hug, lifting her right off her feet.

"Sugar lump!" Faith squealed, hugging him back.

Zoë felt the tiniest twinge of jealousy. Faith had always been so outgoing and friendly. So full of warmth and affection. Why couldn't Zoë be more like that?

Nick set her down and took a good look at her. "Wow. You look great."

"Right back attcha, stud. Zoë was just about to explain why you're staying here. Is something wrong? Did you lose your condo?"

"Um, no," Nick said, looking to Zoë for guidance, like she had the slightest clue how to explain this.

Maybe it would be best to just come right out and say it. "The thing is, I'm pregnant."

Faith's mouth fell open and for about ten seconds she looked too stunned to speak. Maybe just saying it hadn't been the best way to go after all. "You're *what?*"

"Pregnant."

"*Pregnant?* And you didn't *tell* me?"

"Sorry. I was going to call you. I only found out for sure a couple of days ago. I've been a bit… confused."

"Which still doesn't explain what Nick is doing here."

Zoë and Nick looked at each other, then back at Faith. Did they really need to spell it out? Were they so unlikely a couple that Faith would never guess it?

Faith looked from Zoë to Nick, then back to Zoë again. Then she gasped. "It's *Nick's?*"

"You have to swear not to say anything to Mom and Dad," Zoë pleaded. "I haven't decided what to tell them yet."

"How did this happen?" Faith demanded.

"The usual way," Nick said, and Zoë felt her cheeks begin to burn with embarrassment.

"When did you two start seeing each other? And why didn't anyone tell me?"

"Why don't I start dinner while you two talk," Nick said. He beat a path to the kitchen like his pants were in flames and he needed a fire extinguisher.

Coward.

"You and Nick?" Faith said, shaking her head, like she just couldn't believe it.

Zoë felt a jab of annoyance. It's not as if she and

Nick were a different species for God's sake! "Is it really so hard to imagine that Nick would be attracted to someone like me?"

"Of course not. I've always thought you and Nick would be a great couple. I just didn't know you thought so, too."

"I didn't," she admitted. At least not consciously. Maybe all this time the idea had been there, lurking in the back of her mind.

"I want the whole story," Faith said, giving her a pointed look. "And I expect *details*."

Zoë knew exactly what kind of details her sister was referring to.

"Then you had better sit down and get comfortable. This is going to take a while."

Nick, Zoë and Faith sat up until well after midnight chatting. They probably would have stayed up all night if Nick and Zoë hadn't had to go to work the next morning.

Since Nick had the guest room, Faith bunked with Zoë. They took turns in the bathroom, changed into their jammies, then climbed under the covers together, giggling in the dark like they had when they were kids. Back then they'd shared bunk beds. Faith on top and Zoë below.

"Are you sure you can't stay for a few days?" Zoë asked. She didn't see her sister nearly as much as she would have liked to. She wished she lived closer. Especially now that Faith was going to be an aunt.

"I really have to get back. I just had to make sure you were okay. I promised I wouldn't be gone long."

"Promised who?"

Zoë could see the flash of Faith's teeth as she smiled. "I'm seeing someone new. No one really knows about it yet."

"And you accuse me of keeping secrets," Zoë admonished.

"Yeah, well, Mom and Dad aren't exactly going to approve of this, either."

"Let me guess, he's Lutheran."

"Nope."

"Jewish?"

"Atheist."

Zoë cringed. "Ooooh, yikes."

"And he's not a he, he's a she."

For a second Zoë was too surprised to reply. A *she?* "You're dating a *woman?*"

"Are you totally grossed out?" she asked, her voice lacking its usual confidence.

"Of course not! I just…I'm surprised, that's all."

"It kind of surprised me, too."

"What happened? Did you just one day decide, hey, maybe I'll try something new?"

"You know me, I'll try anything once. Her name is Mia. Are you sure it doesn't gross you out?"

She wouldn't lie to herself and not admit it wasn't a little weird to think of her sister in a new way, but all that mattered was that Faith was happy. "I promise, I'm not grossed out."

"That's good, because as strange as it probably sounds, I think I might be in love with her."

It must have been serious, because like Zoë, Faith didn't do love. She didn't let herself get tied down. Didn't talk about having a family. Ever. She just wanted to have fun.

The truth was, Zoë felt jealous. Not about the same sex part. She was firmly rooted in her heterosexuality. She liked men, plain and simple.

What she envied was that Faith had clicked with someone and she went for it, no question. Even though she knew it could potentially get complicated, she wasn't afraid to take a chance.

Why couldn't Zoë be like that? Why couldn't she just open up and let this thing with Nick happen? Why was he sleeping in the guest room when he should have been in bed with her?

"I'm thinking of telling Mom and Dad," Faith said.

"Wow, it must be serious."

"I swear, I've never felt like this about anyone. I know they're going to freak, and possibly disown me. I guess it's a risk I'm willing to take. I feel I owe it to Mia not to try and hide it. I don't want her to think I'm ashamed of our relationship. I'd like you to meet her, too. Maybe we could come down and stay for a couple days."

"I'd like that," Zoë said, and realized she really meant it. She wanted to meet the person that had captured her sister's heart. "Maybe next weekend."

They talked for a while longer, until Faith drifted

off to sleep. Zoë lay there awake until after one, her mind unable to rest. She couldn't stop thinking about all the things that had changed over the past few weeks. She felt as if her entire life had been flipped upside down, spun around and set back down slightly askew.

But not in a bad way. Things would never be the same, but she was beginning to realize that wasn't necessarily a bad thing.

She tossed and turned for another few minutes, then decided to try a glass of warm milk to help her sleep. Which was kind of weird since she'd never in her life had warm milk and the idea sounded pretty gross. She climbed out of bed and tripped over Tucker who lay sleeping on her rug. She couldn't find her slippers in the dark, and she didn't want to disturb her sister by switching on the light, so she padded across the cold floor in bare feet. She headed down the dark stairway but instead of her feet taking her to the kitchen, she found herself standing in the partially open door of the guest room. Maybe that had been her intention all along, and the warm milk was just her way of convincing herself to walk down the stairs in the first place.

She could tell by his slow and deep breathing that Nick was asleep.

Instead of turning around and going to the kitchen, she tiptoed into the room. She had no idea what she was doing, or even why she was doing it. But it wasn't enough to stop her.

Maybe everything wasn't supposed to make

sense. Maybe it was okay to do things simply because it felt good.

Nick was turned away from her, on his right side, his wide shoulders bare. She felt a deep ache in her heart, a pull of longing that propelled her closer to the bed. Closer to him. She wasn't here for sex, she knew that much. She just wanted to be near him.

Without thinking, or considering the consequences, she pulled back the covers and very quietly slipped in beside him. The sheets were cool and soft and smelled of his aftershave.

She rolled onto her side, facing away from him, carefully tucking the covers around her shoulders. Beside her, Nick stirred.

"Zoë?" he said in a voice rough from sleep and rolled toward her.

"Sorry. I didn't mean to wake you."

"S'okay," he mumbled and curled up behind her, enfolding her in the warmth of his body, wrapping a thick arm around her. He spread one large hand over her belly, easing her closer, burying his nose in her hair.

Oh, this was nice.

She held her breath, waiting to see what he would do next, what he would touch, if he would kiss her. And to her surprise, he didn't do a thing. He just snuggled up to her and fell back to sleep. It was as if he knew exactly what she wanted without her even having to ask.

She sighed and placed her hand over his, twining their fingers together. This was definitely more effective than warm milk. Already her lids were beginning to feel heavy. The heat of his body soothed her, his slow, steady breathing warmed the back of her neck and the deep thud of his beating heart lulled her to sleep.

It was a good thing she was having the boss's baby. In any other situation Zoë's erratic work schedule would surely get her fired. And so much for them saving gas driving together.

It was past eleven when she finally strolled into work. Her sister had already been gone by the time she got out of bed, but Faith left a note saying she would call so they could talk about her and Mia visiting next weekend. Nick, she added, had made her breakfast before he left for work.

Zoë hadn't heard or felt him get out of bed. Typically sharing a mattress meant a restless night's sleep for her. Last night, curled up in Nick's arms, she'd slept like the dead and woke feeling well-rested for the first time in weeks.

One very good reason to invite him upstairs to sleep tonight. In fact, maybe it would be better if he moved *all* of his things up there. Maybe it was time to begin treating this exactly the way they should, as an intimate, monogamous relationship between two people who cared deeply for each other. Maybe even loved each other. And if she wasn't actually in love with him yet, she was darned close.

She dropped her purse and jacket in her office

then took the hall down to Nick's office, getting more than a few curious looks and several knowing smiles along the way. News of the kiss had definitely made the rounds. And instead of feeling ashamed or self-conscious, she found herself holding her head a little higher, her back straighter. She found herself answering their looks with a smile that said she was proud to be with a man of Nick's integrity, a man who was so admired by his peers.

If they only knew the *whole* story.

She *wanted* people to know. She was proud to be having Nick's baby.

The thought nearly blew her away.

The only logical explanation was that for years there had been feelings between them that they had either been denying or stowing away. And now that those feelings had been acknowledged and set free, they were multiplying at an exponential rate.

Nick's office was empty, and she remembered belatedly that he had planned to work on-site today— an inspection had been scheduled that he wanted to be there for. She felt a dash of disappointment that she would have to wait all afternoon to see him.

She turned to leave and plowed into a brick wall of a man coming from the opposite direction.

"Whoa!" He grabbed her arms to keep her from toppling over on her butt. She recognized him as O'Connell, the man they had hired only a few weeks ago. The one who'd been giving Nick so much trouble. "Sorry," he said gruffly.

"No, it was my fault." She backed away from him. "I wasn't looking where I was going."

He was *enormous,* with long sandy brown hair, a bushy beard and craggy, almost harsh features. He wore the typical construction worker's uniform— work-faded, dusty jeans, a quilted flannel shirt and steel toed work boots.

"He's not in?" he asked in a deep rumble of a voice.

"No. He's on-site. He should be back sometime later this afternoon."

He gave her a solemn nod and started to walk away, his heavy footsteps vibrating the floor under her feet.

"Can I give you a bit of advice?"

He stopped and turned back to her.

"Nick is a patient man and a fair employer, but you're pushing him over the line."

He narrowed his eyes at her, looking downright fierce. She might have been intimidated, but she'd spent the last ten years around men like him. They looked big and tough, but deep down most were just big teddy bears.

"Is that supposed to scare me?" he asked.

"Your references from your last job were impeccable. Your work is quality. So what's the problem? Why do you keep screwing up?"

"You wouldn't understand," he said gruffly, a distinct hint of sadness lurking behind a pair of piercing blue deep-set eyes. She couldn't help thinking there was more to this situation than he was letting show. And a damned good reason why he was missing work.

She could read people that way.

She propped her hands on her hips and gave him one of her stubborn looks. "Oh yeah, tough guy? Why don't you try me?"

Eight

It was nearly three by the time Nick got back to the office and the only thing on his mind, the only thing that had been on his mind all day, was stopping in to see Zoë. He barely remembered her climbing into bed with him last night, so waking to find her curled in his arms had been a pleasant surprise. And if he hadn't had an appointment with an inspector, he might not have gotten out of bed.

He wasn't going to pretend to know what had motivated her to do it. She was the one calling the shots, setting the pace. But he felt as if they had taken a giant step forward last night.

They had made progress.

He headed into his office to drop off his briefcase

and jacket, and found Zoë sitting at his desk. O'Connell, his problem employee, was standing by the door, as if he'd just been on his way out.

"Nice of you to show up," Nick told him, feeling his good mood fizzle away.

"Boss." O'Connell nodded Nick's way then shot Zoë a half smile. "Thanks."

Nick felt his hackles go up. What the hell was that all about? Why was he smiling at Nick's woman? And why were her eyes red and puffy? Had she been crying?

She sniffled and returned the smile, which pissed off Nick even more. "No problem. You just have to promise you won't make a move until I talk to Nick."

"I won't." He gave her a nod, and ignoring Nick, walked out.

"What was that all about?" Nick demanded. "Why are you crying? Did he hurt you?"

She chuckled and waved away his concerns. "I'm fine. This is nothing. Just the usual overactive hormones."

"What did you need to talk to me about?"

"Come in and shut the door."

He did as she asked and walked over to his desk. "What's going on? I don't like you being alone in here with him. I don't trust him."

A grin split her face. "Nick, are you *jealous?*"

"Of course not," he said automatically, then frowned. Damn, he *was* jealous. He was behaving like a suspicious spouse. "I'm sorry."

"He came in to quit," Zoë told him.

"That's convenient. It'll save me the trouble of firing him."

"I told him I wouldn't let him. And you're not firing him, either."

Maybe she was forgetting who owned the company. "Why the hell not?" he snapped.

"This guy came highly recommended from his last employer. They couldn't say enough good things about him. I knew something had to be up."

"And?"

"So I asked. Like we should have a week ago."

"*And?*" he repeated impatiently.

"And it took some prying, but I finally got him to admit why he's been missing so much work."

No doubt O'Connell had tried to con his way into keeping the job, pulling on Zoë's heartstrings. She was emotionally unstable enough these days to fall for just about anything.

He folded his arms across his chest. "This should be good."

"He has a sick daughter."

Nick frowned. That he hadn't expected. A drug or alcohol problem maybe, but not a sick kid. He didn't even know O'Connell was married. "How sick?"

"She has a rare form of leukemia."

And what if it was all bull? "You're sure he's not just saying that to—"

"He showed me pictures," she interjected, her voice going wobbly and her eyes welling with tears again. "Taken in the children's ward of the hospital. She looks like such a sweet little girl. Only seven years old." She sniffled and wiped away the tears spilling down her cheeks. "Sorry. It was just so sad. He got misty-eyed when he talked about her. I could see how much he loves her, and how hard it's been for him."

Nick cursed and shook his head. "Why the hell didn't he say anything?"

"Because he's a big burly macho guy who thinks he can carry the weight of the world on his shoulders. He lost his wife three years ago, so it's just the two of them. They moved here from up north to be close to Children's Hospital in Detroit. There's a specialist there who thinks he can help her. Only problem is, she has to go in for treatment several times a week and sometimes he can't find anyone to help him. Some days she's so sick from the chemo and radiation he can't leave her."

"I would have given him the days off."

"It gets worse. Even with insurance, medical bills are eating up all his money and they're about to get evicted from the apartment they're staying in. Although from what he says, it sounds like the place is a dump and it's in a terrible neighborhood. He said they have no choice but to go back up north so he can move in with his parents."

"And what about his daughter?"

"This treatment is her last option. Without it she'll probably die."

Nick leaned forward in his seat. "What can we do to help him?"

A grin split Zoë's face. "I talked to him about the company possibly loaning him some money."

"And?"

"He says he's already too far in debt." She plucked a tissue from the box on his desk and wiped the last of her tears away. "I think he's too proud to take a handout."

"We have to do something." There had to be a way to help this guy. A way that wouldn't bruise his pride.

He looked over at Zoë and saw that she was still smiling at him, her eyes full of warmth and affection. "What?"

"You're a good man, Nick."

He shrugged. "Anyone would want to help him."

"No, they wouldn't. But I knew you wouldn't question helping him. You would do it without a second thought."

She got up from his chair and walked to the door. He thought she was going to leave, instead she snapped the lock.

What was she up to?

She turned and started walking toward him, the weeping gone. Instead she gazed down at him a heavy-lidded, almost sleepy look in her eyes. This was awfully familiar. Where had he seen this before...?

Oh yeah, she'd been wearing an identical expression that night in the hotel, seconds before they pounced on each other.

Oh man, here we go again.

Her cheeks were rosy, her lips damp and full, like

plump, dew covered strawberries. He didn't doubt they would be just as sweet and juicy.

She exhaled a breathy sigh and fanned her face. "Phew, it's getting awfully warm in here, isn't it?"

It didn't feel particularly warm to him, although, if she was going to do what he thought she was going to do, it would be a lot warmer in a minute or two. "If you say so."

She reached up, her eyes pinned on his face, and began unfastening the buttons on her shirt. Very slowly, one by one, inch by luscious inch, exposing a narrow strip of pale, creamy skin.

He could see in her eyes, she wanted him. She wasn't doing it because she knew it was what *he* wanted. And she sure wasn't in a hurry.

Well, hell, it *was* getting hot in here.

"I don't want to wait any longer," she said in a husky voice.

"What if someone needs me for something?" he asked, figuring it would be irresponsible to not object at least a little. They were, after all, at work.

"They'll just have to wait their turn."

Well then. He leaned back in his chair to enjoy the show, felt his heart rate skyrocket when she slipped the blouse from her shoulders and let it drop to the floor. Underneath she wore a siren-red transparent lace bra that barely covered the essentials. Her skin looked pale and creamy soft, her nipples taut and nearly as rosy as the fabric that did little to cover them. She wasn't what he would call well-endowed, but what she did have was firm and perfectly shaped. Just enough to fit in his cupped hand with barely any overflow.

And he was so hard that any second he was going to bust out his zipper.

Zoë unfastened her slacks and pushed them down. And when he saw the thong she wore underneath he stopped breathing. In the same vibrant shade as her bra, it was so scandalously brief and transparent it left *nothing* to the imagination.

Had she dressed this way for him or did she always wear sexy underwear to work?

She flashed him a mischievous smile. "See anything you like?"

He lowered his eyes to his crotch, to his very obvious erection. "What do you think?"

He followed the movements of her hand as she stroked a path between the swell of her breasts, trailed it down her taut stomach, stopping briefly to circle her navel, then lower still, brushing her fingers over the itsy bitsy patch of lace.

She leaned forward, resting her hands on the arms of his chair, giving him a beautiful view of her cleavage. "Thinking about stopping me again?"

Oh, hell no. He reached up and hooked a hand behind her neck, pulling her face to his, his fingers tangling through the softness of her pale curls. "Kiss me."

Her lips were soft and warm and so sweet as she brushed them against his own. She slipped into his lap, straddling his thighs, pulling at his clothes—

The knob on his office door rattled, then there was a loud pounding. "Nick! Open up!" John called.

Damn it.

"I'm busy," he shouted in the direction of the door. He had a nearly naked, aroused woman in his lap who seemed intent on getting him naked, too. No way in hell he wasn't going to make love to her.

"It's an emergency."

He closed his eyes, let his head fall back, and cursed.

Zoë let go of the hem of his shirt and called, "What happened?"

There was a brief pause, as Nick was sure his foreman was putting two and two together, then he said, "Sorry to interrupt, but I just got a call that there was an accident at the Troy site."

Zoë sighed and Nick cursed again.

"How bad?" he called.

"I'm not sure. I only know they took one of our guys to the hospital."

He scrubbed his hands across his face and mumbled, "I don't believe this."

"Give us a minute," Zoë said, and he looked up at her apologetically. "I know, you have to go."

She climbed out of his lap and grabbed her clothes from the floor. He stood up and tucked his shirt back in.

He watched her dress, knowing his own face mirrored her look of disappointment. "We have piss-poor timing, don't we?"

She buttoned her blouse and tucked it into her slacks. "No kidding."

As she headed for the door, Nick grabbed her arm and tugged her to him. "Tonight," he said, "you're all mine."

Unfortunately *tonight* never transpired.

Zoë ran home to let the dog out at five, then went back to the office and stayed until eight to make up for some of the time she'd been missing and work she'd been neglecting the past couple of days. She expected Nick to be back home when she pulled in at eight-fifteen, but the driveway was empty and the house dark.

The intense tug of disappointment she felt took her by surprise. Coming home to an empty house had never bothered her before. Well, not usually. Sometimes it sucked being alone, but she always had Dexter to keep her company.

In only a couple of days she'd grown used to having Nick around.

She raided the frozen dinners in the freezer, unable to choose between her two favorites.

"What do you think?" she asked the dog, holding them both up. "Chicken Alfredo or lasagna?"

He looked up at her with a goofy dog smile, his long skinny tail wagging like mad and whacking the table leg.

"You want me to make both?"

He barked, which he almost *never* did, so she took that as a yes. She'd never been much of a dog person, but Tucker wasn't half-bad. She couldn't help growing attached to him, especially when he shadowed her every step, gazing up at her with lovesick puppy eyes.

She nuked both dinners and ate in front of the television, tossing bites to Tucker who gobbled them up enthusiastically. When they were finished eating, Zoë stretched out on the couch with the cat curled up on her feet and the dog sacked out on the rug beside her. She channel surfed, running across a show about babies on the Discovery Channel. She settled in to watch it and the next thing she knew, someone was nudging her awake.

Nine

Zoë pried her eyes open, feeling drugged from sleep. The television was off and Nick stood over her grinning, illuminated only by the light in the hallway.

"What time is it?" she mumbled.

"After midnight."

"I guess I fell asleep." She yawned and stretched. "How did it go at the hospital?"

"Nothing fatal. A couple of cracked ribs and a broken collarbone. He'll be off work for a while, but he'll make a full recovery." He extended a hand toward her. "C'mon, let's get you into bed." At her curious look he added, "To sleep. I think we're both too tired for any fooling around."

He was right. It had been a long eventful day for them both.

He took her hand and hoisted her off the couch.

"Are you coming to bed, too?"

"With you?" he asked, and she nodded. "Do you want me to?"

She really, truly did. "I want you to."

He flashed her that dimpled grin. "Then I will."

"I have to brush my teeth first."

"Me, too. You mind sharing the sink, or do you prefer to take turns?"

It's not as if she had never shared a sink before, and often with three or four other people all rushing to get ready before the school bus honked out front. Besides, that was what couples did, right? "I don't mind."

It was a little weird watching Nick brush his teeth. It was one of those normal everyday things that a person did that she never really thought about, but doing it together felt very personal and intimate. Like learning a secret.

She drew the line at staying in the bathroom while he used the facilities—some secrets should stay secret—and went upstairs to change into her pajamas. In her bedroom she found Tucker and Dexter curled up together on her bed.

She propped her hands on her hips and told Dexter firmly, "You little traitor."

Dexter looked up guiltily.

"Get down," she said, tugging on the covers. Like

new best buddies, both animals jumped off the bed and headed down the stairs together.

It would seem that even Dexter had already adjusted to having them here. That had to be some sort of sign, didn't it?

She stripped down and slipped into an oversized, extra long T-shirt with a Happy Bunny logo on the front. She was already under the covers by the time Nick came upstairs. She curled up on her side and watched as he sat on the edge of the bed and first pulled off his work boots and then his socks. Next he unbuttoned his shirt, tugged it off, and draped it across the footboard.

She sighed with pleasure at the sight of all that beautiful bare skin over ropes of lean muscle. Despite his dark coloring and coarse beard, he wasn't all that hairy. Just a sprinkling on his pecs that trailed down into a narrow path, bisecting his abs and disappearing under the waistband of his jeans.

Looking completely at ease in her bedroom, he rose to his feet and unfastened his jeans. He shoved them down and kicked them off, revealing long powerful legs. Men's legs didn't typically do much for her, but as far as she was concerned Nick's were perfect.

Wearing only his boxers, he slipped into bed beside her. He rolled on his side facing her, leaned close and gave her a brief, but incredibly sweet kiss. His chin felt rough against her skin. He smelled of toothpaste and soap and just a hint of aftershave. "Good night."

"Good night." She reached behind her and

switched off the lamp. As her eyes adjusted to the dark, she could see that Nick had closed his eyes. He must have been pretty tired considering he was typically out of bed before 6 a.m.

Yep, she was tired, too. Absolutely exhausted. Much too tired to finish what they had started in his office this afternoon.

So why couldn't she seem to close her eyes? Why was the urge to touch Nick nagging at her?

She didn't want to wait. She wanted sex now, damn it!

She laid a hand on Nick's arm, rubbing from wrist to shoulder. "Nick, you awake?"

He didn't respond so she gave him a gentle shake. "Nick, wake up."

He answered with a half mumble, half snore.

He was sound asleep.

Swell.

She sighed and rolled onto her back. Two days ago she hadn't been ready for sex, now it was all she could seem to think about. If only they could get their schedules coordinated.

Tomorrow, she decided. Tomorrow they were going to get down and dirty and *nothing* was going to stop them.

"I think I figured out a way to help O'Connell," Nick said the next morning at the breakfast table. He'd fixed them pancakes, sausage patties and freshly squeezed juice from organically grown oranges.

The way she'd been eating lately, she was going to gain a hundred pounds before this baby was done cooking.

"How?" she asked, stabbing her third sausage patty.

"Well, his immediate problem is finding a place to live that he can afford, right? Well, I have a two bedroom condo sitting empty in Royal Oak. They can stay there rent free."

"You're a genius! That's absolutely *perfect*. Do you think he'd go for it?"

"Since it's paid off, and I'm not getting any rent for it now, it's technically not a handout."

"I can't believe we didn't think of it before. And it's even closer to the hospital than the place he's staying in now."

"There's only one possible drawback. Unless I want to kick him and his daughter out at some point, you're going to be stuck with me for God only knows how long."

"And that's okay with you?" she asked.

He nodded. "It really is. How about you?"

She smiled. "It's really okay with me, too."

"You're sure? This is a pretty big step."

A step she honestly felt ready to take. She knew exactly what she wanted, and she was going for it, damn it. "I'm absolutely, and completely sure."

He flashed her that dimpled grin. "Should I talk to O'Connell or do you want to?"

"Since it's your place it would probably be better if you talked to him. It might be easier to accept coming from a guy than me." Then she added, "And you should do it right away."

"Just give me a minute to load the dishwasher," he said, carrying their plates to the sink. "Then we'll get out of here."

Suddenly she couldn't wait to get this settled. After hedging all this time, she was so ready to get Nick moved permanently into her home—into her life—she didn't want to wait another minute.

She followed him to the sink and said, "Nick, look at me."

When he turned to face her, she curled her fingers into the front of his shirt, pulled him down to her level, and gave him a long, deep, wet kiss. One designed to let him know exactly how much she wanted him.

His strong arms circled her, pressing her closer. One big hand plunged through her hair to cup the back of her head while the other traveled downward to fit itself comfortably over her backside.

Zoë pressed her body against him, feeling as if she couldn't get close enough. As if she would *never* be close enough to him.

She knew in that second, without a doubt, she was in love with this man. She was going to marry him, and they were going to have a family. She suddenly understood the appeal of marriage and babies.

Because the babies she had would be Nick's. And it would be his arms she would wake in every morning.

Nick pulled away and flashed her a hungry grin. "Wow, what was that for?"

"It was just a sample of what you have to look forward to later."

He stroked the side of her throat with his thumb, his eyes dark with desire. "I can't wait."

"Me, neither. And the sooner we get to work, the sooner we get to come home."

After only a minimal amount of coercion on Nick's part, and a bit of hedging from O'Connell, he accepted Nick's offer and agreed to move in right away. When O'Connell thanked him, his eyes were filled with such deep gratitude and utter relief, it nearly choked Nick up.

No doubt the guy really loved his little girl. Nick couldn't imagine being in his shoes, the life of his child hanging in the balance. Living with the fear that he couldn't afford the medical treatment needed to save her. Especially after having lost his wife to cancer.

After O'Connell left to pack, Nick sat at his desk thinking about how precious life really was. He tried to imagine it without Zoë. The idea made him sick inside. She was indelibly etched into his life. He had a bond with her that he'd never felt with another woman. That he'd never felt with *anyone*.

"I guess things went well."

Nick looked up to see Zoë standing in his doorway, a big grin on her face. Damn she was pretty. She had that ethereal glow of good health that pregnant women were supposed to have.

She looked…happy.

"What makes you say that?" he asked.

"O'Connell just came up to me in the break room and gave me a bear of a hug and a big kiss." She laughed. "You should have seen the jaws drop. Everyone is going to think I'm cheating on you."

Nick's brow furrowed. "He kissed you?"

"Relax," she said, her grin widening. "It was only on my cheek. And he *smiled*, Nick. Up until that moment I didn't even know he had teeth!"

He didn't like the idea of anyone but him kissing her, but she looked so happy, he felt a grin of his own tugging at the corners of his mouth.

"We really helped him," she said.

He nodded. "We really did."

She crossed the room and slid into his lap, weaving her arms around his neck. "It feels good."

"It certainly does," he growled, tugging her more firmly against him.

She kissed him, drawing his lower lip between her teeth and nibbling. Damn did he love when she did that. She tasted like sweet tea and raspberry-filled donuts.

"Maybe we should lock the door and celebrate," she said, rubbing herself against him. Driving him crazy was more like it. And God it was tempting. After so many near misses, all he had to do lately was look at her and he was instantly hard. He really needed to get this woman into bed. But he wasn't interested in a quickie at the office, when he made love to Zoë, he planned to take his time.

Meaning it would have to wait. *Again.*

"No time," he told her. "We have to get over to my condo and pack up my things. I told him he could move in right away."

She gave him an adorable little pout, then sighed and said, "Well then, I guess we had better hurry. And I don't care if we don't get home until 2 a.m., we are getting naked tonight."

Sounded like a good plan to him.

It was after eight when they finally got Nick's things loaded in the back of his truck and headed home.

Home. The word had a totally different meaning to her now.

While helping him pack, Zoë made a startling and somewhat disturbing discovery. Nick had no pictures from his childhood, no family mementos. Nothing to indicate he even had a family. It was as if he had no past at all, or at least not one he had any desire to look back on.

She had boxes and boxes of photos and old birthday cards, pictures her younger siblings had drawn for her, and even a couple of their baby teeth. She had at least one or two items from each member of her family.

Only then did it truly sink in, did she realize what it must have been like for him growing up. How lonely he must have been, and why having a family was so important to him now.

He'd never truly experienced a *real* family and now she wanted to be the one who gave him that. She wanted to be the one who finally made him feel complete. She planned to spend the rest of her life making up for every lonely day, every isolated minute he had ever spent. Even if that meant having another baby. Or even a third.

Which, of course, would necessitate them getting a bigger house. She wondered if he would mind moving into a more rural setting. Maybe Romeo or Armada. They could have a huge yard for Tucker and the kids to play in. She could have an enormous flower garden, and maybe start growing vegetables. She could can pickles and jam, the way her grandmother used to. Maybe she could even take an extended leave from work and try the stay-at-home-mom thing for a while. Or at the very least work part time from home.

A world of opportunities she'd never even considered had opened up to her and she couldn't wait to see just where life would lead her.

"You're awfully quiet," Nick said, as he backed his truck into the driveway and parked beside her car. "Everything okay?"

She turned to him and smiled. "I'm just conserving my energy for other things."

He put the truck in park and killed the engine. "I want to say to hell with the unloading, but everything I own is sitting back there. I could probably just toss it all into the garage."

"The lock on the door is broken." It wasn't as if she lived in a bad neighborhood. Birmingham was considered upscale by most accounts, but there was no point taking chances. "If we move fast, we can get the boxes unloaded in no time. Consider it foreplay."

"You don't pick up anything heavier than a phone book," he said firmly and she rolled her eyes. He was such a guy.

They climbed out and he opened the tailgate while she unlocked the front door. She could hear Tucker inside, hopping around excitedly like an overgrown rabbit. They had stopped by home only a couple of hours ago to feed him and let him out, but he greeted her as if she'd been gone for days.

"I know, I know," she said, patting his head as she pushed her way through the door. "We missed you, too, you big oaf."

She grabbed Tucker's collar so he wouldn't bolt and held the door open for Nick. He brushed past her with two boxes marked Bedroom. He carried them down the hall and past the stairs.

"Where are you going with those?" she asked.

He turned to her, a puzzled look on his face. "To the bedroom."

"But our bedroom is upstairs."

A slow grin curled his mouth. "*Our* bedroom."

"Our bedroom," she repeated. And because she knew what was coming next, she added, "And yes, I'm sure."

Savoring the mildly stunned, incredibly happy expression on his face, she headed out the door to grab more boxes. If he thought he was happy now, he should just wait until she'd gotten her hands on him.

After she was through with him, a bulldozer couldn't pry the smile from his face.

"That's it," Nick said, closing and locking the front door.

They had hauled everything inside in under twenty minutes and the anticipation was killing her.

Now it was time to get to the good stuff.

"You know what that means," Zoë said, looking up at him from under lids that were already heavy with pent-up lust. Her legs and arms felt warm and weak and her head felt dizzy. She couldn't recall a time in her life when she'd been more turned on by the idea of making love to someone.

She took off her jacket and tossed it over the back of the couch. With a look to match her own, Nick did the same.

As she pulled her shirt up over her head, every inch of her skin buzzed with sexual awareness. The brush of lace from her bra teased her already sensitive nipples. The vee of skin between her thighs ached to be caressed. Even her hair felt alive and tingly.

Nick yanked his shirt over his head and dropped it on the floor. His skin looked deep golden tan in the dim lamplight. Her heart tapped out a wild beat as he walked toward her, unfastening his jeans. She couldn't wait to get her hands on him, touch and taste every inch. How could she have denied herself this? Why hadn't she realized how good it would be?

He stopped in front of her and she felt dizzy with

anticipation, every cell screaming to be touched. He lowered his head to kiss her and she rose up on her toes to meet him halfway. Their lips touched and she went hot all over, as if someone had replaced the blood in her veins with liquid fire.

He unfastened her jeans, shoving them down and she stopped kissing him just long enough to wiggle out of them and kick them into the dark corner beside the couch.

Her heart beat harder, in perfect time with the sudden loud pounding on the front door.

Nick groaned and pressed his forehead to hers, his breath coming hard and fast. "I don't *believe* this."

She didn't have a clue who it could be this time of night, but whatever they wanted couldn't possibly be as important as her getting into Nick's pants this very second.

"They'll go away." She slipped her hand inside his open fly and stroked the firm ridge of his erection through his boxers. He closed his eyes and groaned. He lifted her right off her feet and backed her against the wall separating the kitchen from the living room. She hooked her legs over his hips and gasped as the length of his erection rocked against her, her breasts crushed into his chest.

She kissed him and his mouth tasted hot and tangy. She felt as if she couldn't get enough, as though she could eat him alive and crawl all over him. She clawed at his jeans, shoving them and his boxers down, then cupped his bare behind, digging her nails into his flesh, feeling wild and sexy and completely out of control. No man had ever made her want to let go this way, to give so much of herself.

The pounding on the door persisted for a minute or two, then through a haze of arousal Zoë heard the jingle of keys, and the rattle of the doorknob being turned. Nick must have heard it too because he stopped kissing her and went stone still.

It happened so fast, neither had time to react. One minute they were alone, the next her sister was standing in the open doorway staring at them, mouth agape. Thank goodness there weren't many lights on, but there was no mistaking exactly what was happening.

For several seconds time stood still. No one moved or said a word. Faith looked down at Zoë's hands, still clutching Nick's behind. She said, "Nice ass," then burst into tears and walked back out the door.

Ten

"**I**'m so sorry," Faith hiccupped for the umpteenth time since Nick and Zoë had yanked their clothes on and tugged her back inside the house. Zoë sat on the couch by Faith. Nick stood across the room wearing a typical male slightly confused, mildly alarmed expression, looking as though any second he might bolt.

Faith was not the crying type, not even when she was a kid, which led Zoë to believe something really awful had happened. At first Faith had been crying too hard to string together a coherent sentence. They were only able to assess that she wasn't in need of medical attention and no one had died.

Faith sniffled and tugged another tissue from the box in her lap. "I can't believe I fell apart like that, and I really can't believe I walked in on you right in the middle of…well, you know."

"Stop apologizing," Zoë told her. "Tell us what happened."

Faith wiped away the mascara smudges under her eyes. "I am such an idiot."

Nick pushed off the wall where he'd been leaning. "Why don't I leave you two alone to talk."

Before Zoë or Faith could answer, he was on his way up the stairs.

"Wow," Faith said. "I sure scared him off."

Zoë shrugged. "What can I say, he's a guy. He's been getting more than his share of emotional stuff from me these days. I think he's suffering from an overload."

Faith sat there for a second, quietly toying with the tissue, then she looked up at Zoë and said, "I got dumped."

"Oh, Faith." Zoë rubbed her sister's shoulder.

As if Tucker could sense her unhappiness and wanted to help, he walked over to the couch and laid his head in Faith's lap, gazing up at her with what Zoë could swear was a look of sympathy.

Faith sniffled and scratched him behind the ears. "I told her I loved her, and I wanted us to move in together. I told her I was going to tell my parents the truth, no matter the consequences, and she told me I probably didn't want to do that. Then she said she decided to go back to her husband."

"I didn't know that she was married."

"Neither did I. Long story short, Mia said she had

just been experimenting, and basically trying to make her husband jealous. And I guess it worked. He wants her back." Faith sniffled and wiped away fresh tears. "She was so…*cold*. Like she never cared about me at all. Like I was some high school science experiment."

"Oh, sweetie, I'm so sorry. I know how much you cared about her."

"I feel so stupid. But I can't help thinking I deserved this."

That was just crazy. "How could you possibly deserve to be treated this way?"

"Do you know how many men I've dumped who claimed to 'love' me?"

"Honey, you deserve to be happy just as much as anyone else."

"Speaking of being happy," Faith said, brightening. "It looks like things with you and Nick are going pretty well, huh?"

Zoë felt guilty admitting how happy she was in light of her sister's heartache, but she couldn't contain her joy. "I'm going to tell him yes. I'm going to marry him."

"Oh my gosh!" Faith squealed excitedly and gave her a big hug. "I can't think of a more perfect man for you." She held Zoë at arm's length and grinned. "Not to mention that he has a mighty find rear end."

Zoë grinned. "No kidding."

"Speaking of that, I should go and let you guys get back to business. I can stay in a hotel."

"You're not staying in a hotel. The spare bedroom is free now. Stay as long as you like."

"I don't have to be to work until Monday, so maybe I will hide out here for a couple of days, if you don't mind."

"We would love to have you," Zoë said, rising from the couch, anxious to get upstairs and finish what she and Nick had started. "Maybe we can go shopping tomorrow. Spending money always helps me chase away a bad mood."

"Just so you know, I'll be sleeping with these on." She held up a pair of headphones and an MP3 player, and grinned mischievously. "So be as loud as you like. I won't hear a thing."

When Zoë finally made it upstairs, Tucker on her heel, Nick was sitting in bed, bare-chested and gorgeous, reading a hardcover novel.

"Everything all right?" he asked.

"She got dumped."

"That's kind of what I figured." He closed the book and set it on the nightstand. "Is she okay?"

"Bruised but not broken." She peeled her shirt off and tossed it in the general direction of the hamper, missing her target by several feet. "I hope you don't mind, but she's going to stick around for a couple days. I don't think she wants to be alone."

"Of course I don't mind. But I guess that nixes tonight's scheduled activities, huh?"

She peeled off her jeans and dropped them

where she stood. "I don't care if the house burns down, nothing is going to stop me from getting you naked tonight."

"That's convenient." He flashed her a sexy, dimpled grin, and tossed back the covers. "Because I'm already naked."

Holy moly! Naked and *very* aroused. She raised a brow at him. "Did you start without me?"

"It won't go away. I need you to put me out of my misery."

"It would be my pleasure." She walked around to his side of the bed, dropping her bra and panties along the way. The way his eyes raked over her—she felt as if she were the sexiest, most desirable woman on the planet.

He patted his thighs. "Come'ere."

She climbed in his lap, straddling him. His crisp leg hair tickled her skin as she lowered herself onto his thighs. His body felt warm and solid as he looped an arm around her waist and drew her closer.

"Here we are," he said, tucking her hair back behind her ears.

Finally. "Just you and me."

He stroked her cheek, his eyes searching her face. "I want you to know that there is no one else on earth that I would rather be with right now. That I would *ever* want to be with."

His words warmed her from the inside out. There was no one she would rather be with, either. "Me, too."

She still wanted him, couldn't wait to feel him

inside her again, but that sense of urgency was gone. Now she wanted to take her time, savor every minute. He must have felt the same way, because for the longest time they only played with each other, kissing and stroking and tasting. Exploring each other as if it was the first time, yet she felt as if they had learned each other a hundred years ago.

How could something be exciting and new, yet this comfortable and familiar?

"I love the way this feels," he said, using his thumbs to gently caress the smooth skin at the junction of her thighs. He watched his movements, as if he found the sight of it fascinating. His featherlight strokes made her hot and cold at the same time and her head started getting that dizzy, detached feeling.

She rose up on her knees to give him a better look, gripping the headboard on either side of him and he groaned his appreciation.

He leaned forward, his hair brushing against her stomach and touched her with his tongue. Just one quick flick, but his mouth was so hot, the sensation so shockingly intense, she gasped with surprise and jerked away.

He looked up, a grin on his face, and said, "Delicious."

She might have been embarrassed, but she was too turned on. He cupped her behind in his big, warm hands and pulled her back to his mouth, lapping and tasting while she balanced precariously between torture and bliss. Every slow, deep stroke of his tongue took her higher, until she could hardly stand it. She wanted to grab his head and push him deeper.

She wanted more, and at the same time she was on total sensory overload.

She was aware of the sound of her own voice, but the words were jumbled and incoherent. The wet heat of his tongue, the rasp of his beard stubble on her bare skin—it was too much.

The pleasure started somewhere deep inside, in her soul maybe, and radiated outward. It gripped her with such momentum, time seemed to grind to an abrupt halt. Every muscle in her body clenched tight and her eyes clamped shut. Her hands tangled in his hair, trapping him close as she rode the waves of pleasure. Her body shook and quaked for what felt like forever.

Her heart throbbed in time with the steady pulse between her thighs. She didn't know if it was Nick's incredible skills or the pregnancy hormones, or maybe even a combination of both, but she had never come so hard in her entire life.

She sank down into his lap and rested her forehead against his shoulder, wanting to tell him how out-of-this-world, amazingly and unbelievably sensational he'd just made her feel, how she was pretty sure she'd just had her first out-of-body experience, but she was barely able to breathe much less use her mouth to form words.

So instead, she kissed him, tasting herself on his

lips and finding it unbelievably erotic. She reached down between them and wrapped her fingers around the impressive girth of his erection. He groaned low in his chest and kissed her harder.

She stroked him slowly, felt him pulse in her hand. He was hot to the touch and velvet smooth. She wanted to take him into her mouth, but when she made a move to bend forward he caught her head in his hands, tangling his fingers through her hair. "Don't."

"I want to."

"I want to make love to you."

"Can't we do both."

He shook his head. "I'm so hot for you right now, it's going to have to be one or the other, and I need to be inside of you."

Well, if he put it that way. Besides, what was the rush? They had the rest of their lives to try anything they wanted. And though she had never been particularly creative or adventurous in bed, she wanted to try it all with Nick.

"You know the best thing about pregnant sex?" he asked wrapping his hands around her hips.

"Huh?"

He fed her a mischievous grin. "No need for a condom."

Nick guided her and she lowered herself on top of him. He sank inside her slow and smooth and oh so deep.

He hissed out a breath, his grip on her tightening. For a moment they sat that way, not moving, barely even breathing. It was almost scary what a perfect fit they were, how connected she felt to him. There was no doubt in her mind that Nick was the man she was supposed to spend the rest of her life with. She wanted to have babies with him and grow old with him.

And she wanted him to know exactly how she was feeling. "Nick, I love you."

He smiled, caught her face between his hands and kissed her, tender and sweet. And she couldn't stop her body from moving, from rising and sinking in a slow, steady rhythm. She watched with fascination as a look of pure ecstasy washed over his face. He let her set the pace, let her do most of the work while he kissed and touched her and whispered sexy, exciting things to her. She found herself answering him, using words she never would have expected to come out of a good Catholic girl's mouth. Dirty things he seemed to love hearing.

He reached between them, caressing the sensitive bud he had so skillfully manipulated with his tongue, and the reaction was instantaneous. Pleasure slammed her from all sides, hard, deep and intense. Forget an out-of-body experience. She wasn't even on the same planet. Only when she heard Nick groan her name, when his body rocked up to meet hers, did she realize she'd taken him along for the ride.

They sat there for several minutes afterward, catching their breath. She kept telling herself she should move, but he was still hard and he felt so good inside her. She waited, watching the minutes tick by on the alarm clock, two, then three, then five, but it still didn't go away. In fact, instead of getting soft, she was pretty sure he was getting harder.

Just for fun, she wiggled her hips and he answered her with a rumble of pleasure.

"You weren't kidding about it not going away." She sat up and smiled. "I'm impressed."

"You know what that means," he said, returning her smile. "We'll just have to do it again."

"Do you remember when we first met?" Nick asked. Zoë lay in his arms her head resting against his chest. She smelled so warm and sweet and girly. It was getting late, and they both had to get up and go to work, but his mind was moving a million miles an hour.

"Of course. I came for an interview, and did a pretty fair job of lying through my teeth."

He played with her hair, looping a curl around his index finger then letting it spring free. There were so many places on her body to play with, so many things to touch. He was pretty sure that tonight he'd managed to play with or touch just about every single one. As far as sex went, Zoë didn't seem to have a single reservation or hang-up. He could do or try pretty much anything and she was always ready for more. Things so forbidden and intimate he'd never had the guts to try them so early in a relationship. Of course, they'd had ten years to develop a deep sense of trust.

It had just taken them a while to get to the good stuff.

"I knew an eighteen-year-old couldn't possibly

have the experience you listed on your application, but you looked so young and vulnerable. I couldn't turn you away."

She looked up at him. "Are you saying you took pity on me?"

He grinned. "Pretty much, yeah."

She propped her chin on his chest. "As much as I wanted to get away from my family, those first few months were hard. I never anticipated how lonely I would be. You were incredibly patient with me considering how bad I stunk as a secretary."

He chuckled. "But you tried so hard, I didn't have the heart to fire you. I knew deep down that you were special. And you were cute."

"I never told you this, but I had a major crush on you for the first year."

"I could kind of tell."

She looked surprised. "Really?"

"Yeah, and I was tempted, believe me. But at the time I wasn't looking for a relationship, and I didn't want to risk killing our friendship with a one-night stand. I liked you too much."

"Want to hear something weird. Almost every boyfriend I've had over the years has felt threatened by my relationship with you."

"Want to hear something even weirder? I've had the same problem with *every* one of my girlfriends. It was as if they couldn't believe a guy like me could have a woman as a good friend."

"Maybe they were seeing something we didn't."

"Maybe." He stroked the wispy curls back from her face. "I never told you what Lynn said right before our wedding, the real reason she decked me."

"What did she say?"

"As we were getting out of the car in the courthouse parking lot, she told me that she would only marry me if I fired you."

Zoë's eyes widened. "You're kidding!"

"She didn't want me seeing you anymore, either. I had to break all ties with you."

"That's crazy. What did you say?"

"At first I thought she was joking, and when I realized she was serious, I was too stunned to say anything. It's not as if I wasn't already having major doubts, but up until that moment I had really planned to go through with it."

"Yet, you waited until the last minute to dump her."

"She was so…manipulative. I guess I wanted to punish her, or knock her down a few pegs at least. You should have seen the smug look on her face when we were standing there. When I backed out, I was more or less saying that I was choosing you over her."

"That had to sting." She sounded sympathetic, but he could tell she was getting a lot of satisfaction from this. She liked hearing that he'd picked her over the woman he'd asked to marry him.

"I'm ashamed to admit it, but I actually enjoyed dumping her."

"That makes two of us, because I enjoyed it, too."

"Now I'm exactly where I'm supposed to be." He

spread his hand over her flat belly, where their child was growing. "Here with you and the baby."

Zoë sighed and rested her head on Nick's chest, cupping her hand over his. So was she, exactly where she belonged. And she wanted to tell him so, right now. But after making him wait for an answer to his marriage proposal, somehow just saying yes didn't seem good enough.

Nick," she said, stroking the tops of his fingers.

"Huh?"

"Would you marry me?"

He was silent, so she looked up and saw that he was grinning. A great big dimpled grin full of love and affection. He had gotten the message loud and clear. He leaned forward, caught her face in his hands and kissed her. *"Absolutely."*

A part of her sighed with relief. Not that she thought he was going to say no. Maybe it was because things were finally settled, it felt as though her life was back on track.

Yet there was something else. A niggling in the back of her mind. A tiny seed of doubt. "I think we should do it soon," She said, feeling a sudden urgency to get this settled. To get on with their life together. Like maybe deep down she thought he might change her mind. "You know, because of the baby."

"How soon?"

"How does next Friday work for you?"

His smile got even bigger. "Friday would be perfect."

"Something really small, like the justice of the peace?"

"Whatever you want."

She settled into his arms and snuggled against him, knowing deep down to her soul that she was doing the right thing, and hoping he felt the same way.

He was quiet for several minutes then asked, "Can I tell you a secret?"

"You can tell me anything."

"I've never once told anyone I love them."

She propped herself up on her elbow to look at him. His eyes were so…*sad*. "How is that possible? You were engaged two times."

"Weird huh?"

"You didn't love them?" A part of her wanted him to say he hadn't. The selfish part that wanted him to love only her.

"I don't know. Maybe I did in my own way. Maybe I'm not physically capable."

Maybe growing up the way he had, had damaged him somehow. How terribly sad that a person could go through their entire life never feeling real love.

"I'm a different person with you, Zoë. We're going to be a family."

She let her head drop back down, breathed in the scent of him, felt his heart thump against her ear.

A family. Her and Nick.

Did that mean he loved her? And if he did, why didn't he say the words? Was he really not capable?

Or was admitting that to her just the first step? And

if it had been, at least it was a step in the right direction.

He was quiet for a while, then his breathing became slow and steady and she knew he had fallen asleep.

He did love her. And it wasn't just wishful thinking. She knew it in her heart. She sensed it when he looked at her, could feel it when he touched her. When he was ready, he would tell her.

She would just have to be patient.

Eleven

Zoë felt like death warmed over the next morning at seven when Nick nudged her awake. She managed to pry one eye open far enough to see that he was already showered and dressed and far too awake considering how late they had fallen asleep. And it must have been pretty obvious that she was in no shape to go to work, because he just kissed her, tucked the covers up over her shoulders and said he would see her later.

She fell back to sleep and had strange, disturbing dreams. She dreamed it was her wedding day, and she was walking down the aisle, her arm looped in her father's. Instead of a white gown, she wore the dress she'd worn to both of Nick's weddings, complete with broken straps and stains, and it had been dyed crimson—the same shade as her sister's car.

Not that anyone seemed to think that was out of the ordinary. Row upon row of people dressed in white sat on either side smiling and nodding. Bunches of blood-red roses decorated the aisle, giving everyone a pale, ethereal look.

Her mind kept telling her that everything was normal, but something didn't feel right.

She could see Nick waiting for her by the altar, wearing the same suit he'd worn at his last wedding. He was smiling, but it looked unnatural and plastic, as if he was being forced to stand there against his will. She kept walking toward him, telling herself everything was going to be okay, but instead of getting closer, the longer she walked, the farther away he was getting. The cloying scent of roses crowded the air. But instead of smelling like flowers, it smelled metallic, like blood. It burned her nose and made her stomach ache.

Something definitely wasn't right.

She started walking faster, trying desperately to reach him, but Nick was fading from her vision. Disappearing. She called out to him, but he didn't seem to hear her.

She broke into a run but her legs felt heavy and weak and cramps knotted her insides, doubling her over. The fog grew thicker, closing in around her like wet paper. She clawed her way through it, felt it filling her lungs, constricting her air. She couldn't see, couldn't breathe, could hear nothing but the frantic pounding of her heart.

She called for him again but it was no use. Nick and her father, the smiling people, they were all gone. She was all alone with the sick feeling that she'd just become number three. Nick had left her at the altar, just like the others.

She felt a firm hand on her shoulder and someone called her name.

Zoë shot up in bed, disoriented and out of breath.

"Hey, you okay?" Faith stood beside the bed, a look of concern on her face.

"Bad dream." Her voice sounded weak and scratchy.

"You called for Nick. He already left for work." She touched Zoë's forehead. "You're all sweaty."

Faith was right. The sheet was clinging to her damp skin and her hair felt wet. She felt hot and cold at the same time and everything was fuzzy and surreal.

Zoë blinked several times and fought to pull herself awake, but couldn't shake the sensation of being caught somewhere between sleep and consciousness. It took a minute to realize that the cramps in her stomach hadn't faded with the dream.

It wasn't real, she told herself. She was fine. But the pain was very real and too intense.

Fear skittered across her spine, and her heart gave a violent jolt in her chest.

Faith looked downright scared now. "Zoë, what's wrong? You're white as a sheet."

Everything was fine. The baby was fine, she assured herself, but the tips of her fingers had begun to go numb with fear. She felt as if she couldn't pull in a full breath.

That was when Zoë felt it. The warm gush between her legs.

No, this was not happening.

She and Nick were going to get married. They were going to have a baby together.

"Zoë?" Faith's hand was on her shoulder again and there was real fear in her voice. "Talk to me."

The pain intensified, cramps gripped deeper.

No, no, no, this couldn't be happening. She had to find a way to stop it. She had to *do* something.

She looked up at her sister, tears welling in her eyes. "I think I'm losing the baby."

Nick stood impatiently waiting for the hospital elevator to reach the third floor. He didn't have a clue what was going on, only a message from Faith telling him to get to Royal Oak Beaumont Hospital.

He'd been out of the office all morning, and because he had forgotten to charge it last night, his cell phone was dead. He was unaware of any problem until twenty minutes ago when Shannon accosted him on his way to his office.

He'd tried both Faith's and Zoë's cell phones before he left but neither was answering.

There had to be some rational explanation, he kept telling himself. Nothing was wrong. He was sure that she was fine.

And still a knot of fear had lodged itself in his gut. What if she wasn't fine? What would he do then?

The elevator dinged and the doors slid open. He

crossed the hall to the nurses' station and gave the nurse, an older woman with a fatigued face, Zoë's name.

"Room thirteen-forty," she said in a voice that mirrored her tired expression. She motioned with a jerk of her thumb. "That way, around the corner."

He started down the hall, his heart beating faster and harder with every step.

She was fine. Everything would be okay.

He rounded the corner and saw Faith standing outside one of the rooms. When she turned and saw him coming, he could see by the expression on her face that everything was *not* okay.

His heart took a sudden dive and landed with a plop in the pit of his stomach.

"What happened," he demanded. "Is Zoë okay?"

"She's fine," Faith said. "They're going to keep her overnight just to be safe."

Relief hit his so hard and swift his knees nearly buckled. He braced a hand against the door frame to steady himself. He hadn't realized until just then how scared he'd been. He didn't know what he would have done if she'd been hurt or sick.

So why was she here?

Then it hit him. He'd been so worried about Zoë, he'd completely forgotten about the pregnancy.

"The baby?" he asked.

Faith paused and bit her lip, looking exactly like Zoë did when something was wrong.

Damn it.

They had lost the baby.

What was this going to do to Zoë? Lately she had really warmed to the idea of becoming a mother. He knew this was going to be tough for her to handle. She would feel so guilty. And what if it had something to do with last night? He would never forgive himself if this was his fault.

Right now, he just needed to see for himself that Zoë was okay. "Can I go in?"

"Of course. She's been waiting for you."

Taking a deep breath, he walked past Faith into the room. Zoë sat in the bed wearing a hospital gown looking so small and vulnerable. So alone and numb.

"Hey," he said, walking over to the bed. As he got closer, he could see that she was holding back tears, fighting to keep it together.

It was just like her to think she had to be strong for everyone else.

She looked up at him, her eyes so full of hurt. "We lost the baby."

He had known, but hearing the words felt like a stab in his gut.

"She told me. I'm so sorry I didn't get here sooner." He sat on the edge of the bed and she sat stiffly beside him. She was so tense, one good poke would probably snap her in half. Did she think he was going to make her go through this alone?

"I'm so sorry," she whispered, her voice trembling.

"Zoë, it's okay. It's not your fault." He put an arm around her and nudged her toward him, and everything in her seemed to let go. A soft sob racked through her and she dissolved into his arms. She cried quietly for several minutes and he just held her. He had no idea what to say, what to do. He didn't even know what had happened.

"I-I thought you might be mad," she finally said, her voice quiet and miserable.

He grabbed a tissue and handed it to her. "Why would I be mad?"

She shrugged and wiped away the tears. "I know how much you wanted this."

"But your being okay means a lot more to me."

"It's so weird. I was so freaked out about being pregnant, now I feel so…empty. I really wanted this baby, Nick."

"I know you did." He stroked back a stray curl that clung to her damp cheek. He didn't even want to know, but he had to ask. "Do they know what caused it? I mean, last night…"

"It wasn't that. They did an ultrasound and I could tell by the look on her face that the technician saw something wrong, but she wouldn't say what. She said the doctor would be in soon to see me. That was like an hour ago."

"I'm so sorry I wasn't here for you." Nick rubbed her back soothingly. Sometimes he forgot how petite she was. How vulnerable. His first instinct was to protect her. To say anything to make her hurt less. "I'm sure everything is fine."

"What if it isn't?" she said, sounding genuinely frightened. "What if something is really wrong? I thought I never wanted kids, but the idea of never being able to—" Her voice hitched.

"There's no point in worrying until we know what's going on."

But that got Nick thinking, what if she couldn't have kids? What if they could *never* have a child together? After all these years of longing for a family, waiting for just the right time, could he marry a woman who was infertile?

The answer surprised him.

The truth was, it didn't make a damned bit of difference, if the woman he was marrying was Zoë. Maybe at first his desire to marry her was partially due to the pregnancy, but not any longer. He wanted her.

Baby or no baby.

Before he could tell her that, Doctor Gordon walked in, Faith on his heels. Zoë wrapped her hand around his and squeezed. He could feel her trembling.

"First, I just went over the results of the ultrasound. I want to assure you that neither of you is in any way at fault. There is a thin membrane that has separated Zoë's uterus into two sections. This constricted the baby's growth, causing the miscarriage."

He went on to explain that she was actually lucky that the egg had implanted itself on the smaller side. Had it been on the other side it's quite possible she could have progressed well into the fourth or even fifth month before miscarrying, which would have been a much more devastating loss.

Nick found it tough to think of losing a baby as a good thing, but what the doctor said made sense.

Zoë didn't say anything, just kept a death grip on his hand, so Nick asked what he knew she was probably afraid to. "Is this something you can fix?"

"I can perform a simple outpatient procedure to remove the membrane," he said. "With no complications, recovery time is usually only a week or two."

"And then she'll be okay? She'll be able to get pregnant?" He wanted to know more for Zoë's sake than his own. He didn't want any question in her mind.

"Did you have any difficulty conceiving?"

"Nope," Zoë and Nick said in unison and the doctor cracked a smile. Getting pregnant had been the easy part.

"Then I see no reason why, with the surgery, she wouldn't be able to conceive and carry a baby to term." He flashed Zoë a reassuring smile. "I think you're going to be just fine."

The grip on Nick's hand eased. He could almost feel the relief pouring through her. He knew how doctors worked. In this litigious society they didn't give false hope. Zoë would be okay. They would get past this. She would have the surgery and they could try again.

"I'd like to see you in the office in two weeks," Doctor Gordon told Zoë. "If everything looks good we can schedule the procedure."

Zoë and Nick each asked a few more questions, then thanked him. When he was gone, Faith walked around the bed and gave Zoë a big hug and a kiss on the cheek. "I'm glad everything is okay."

"Thanks," Zoë said, and some unspoken understanding seemed to pass between them.

She had no idea how lucky she was to have that kind of bond with someone. To have family. Now he would know, too. When they got married, her family would be his.

"I'm going to run down to the cafeteria and give you guys some time alone," Faith told them. "I'll see you in a bit."

After she left, Zoë said, "So, I guess you're off the hook, huh?"

She couldn't possibly mean what he thought she meant. Nick took her hand and held it. "Which hook would that be?"

"There's no baby. You don't have to marry me now."

"I'm going to pretend you didn't say that."

"What if I can't have another baby, Nick?"

"That's too bad, sweetheart. You're stuck with me." A tear rolled down her cheek and he brushed it away with his thumb. "You heard what the doctor said. There's no reason to worry about that now. You'll have the surgery and everything will be fine."

She nodded, but didn't look completely convinced.

"There is something missing, though," he said.

She frowned. "Missing?"

"We still have to make it official." Enjoying her puzzled look, he reached into his jacket pocket and pulled out the small velvet box. He lifted the lid and watched her jaw drop when she saw the two carat marquee cut platinum diamond engagement ring that had taken him three hours at six different jewelers to choose.

"Oh my God," she breathed, looking genuinely stunned. "You got me a ring?"

"Yeah, and it took me all morning to find the perfect one." He took the ring from its satin bed. She held her breath as he slipped it on the ring finger of her right hand. It was a perfect fit. Feminine but not too flashy.

She held up her hand and the stone shimmered in the fluorescent lights. "How did you know what size?"

"I borrowed a ring from your jewelry box before I left this morning. Do you like it?"

"It's exactly what I would have chosen." Tears welled in her eyes. Happy ones, he hoped. Then she looked up at him with a watery smile. "It's perfect, Nick."

"So now it's official. And since there's no rush, we can wait and plan something nice if you want. Something bigger. I hear most women spend their lives planning their wedding day."

She shook her head. "Not me. I don't need a big wedding. And I don't want to wait. I want to do it next Friday, like we planned."

"Are you sure you'll be feeling up to it? You've been through a lot today—"

"I feel better already knowing everything is going to okay. I want to try again as soon as the doctor says it's safe. I want us to have a baby."

He squeezed her hand. "Whatever you want."

"And I want more than one. At least two, maybe even three."

Wow. When she changed her mind, she really did a complete one-eighty. "We'll never fit a family of five into your house or my condo. I'll have to build us something bigger."

"With a yard big enough for Tucker and the kids to play in? And a huge garden?"

"Whatever you want."

"That's what I want," she said, wrapping her arms around him and hugging him tight. "That's exactly what I want."

She looked happy, and sounded happy, so why did Nick get the feeling something wasn't right?

Twelve

Zoë took the rest of the week off and though Nick thought she needed more time, she was tired of sitting around feeling sorry for herself and went back to work Monday morning.

It had been the right thing to do. Four days later she felt as though she had begun to heal both physically and mentally. She felt ready to move on.

She kept reminding herself what the doctor said, how much worse it would have been if she'd been four or five months along. The baby would have been almost fully developed. A little person. They would have known if it was a boy or a girl.

And they would have spent the days following

the miscarriage not recovering, but planning a funeral. The idea gave her a cold chill.

So really, losing the baby so early, when it was just a speck of life she hadn't even felt move, was a blessing in disguise.

As badly as Nick wanted children, she had expected him to be really upset, but he had seemed more concerned about her health than the fact that they had lost a child. Not that he hadn't made it clear he was concerned about future fertility issues, and he seemed so relieved when the doctor said the surgery would probably fix the problem.

She couldn't help wondering, what if it didn't? Nick hadn't even been willing to discuss it. What if something went wrong and she could never have kids? How would Nick feel about marrying her then?

Of course, by then they would already be married.

Maybe that was why he'd suggested putting the wedding off for a while. Maybe he wanted to be sure she was okay before he tied himself down to her. Maybe he didn't want to marry a woman who couldn't give him children.

She closed her eyes and shook her head.

That was ridiculous. He'd gotten her a beautiful ring and he'd been unbelievably sweet the past few days.

At the hospital, all she had wanted was to come home, but when she got home, it felt as though everything had changed. Getting back to her regular routine had been so difficult. He had stayed beside her the entire first day after it happened. He'd brought her tea and held her when she cried, which was almost constantly.

Why would he do any of that if he didn't want to marry her? If he didn't love her?

And if he did love her, why didn't he say it?

"Hey Zoë, how ya feeling?"

Zoë looked up to find Shannon standing in her office doorway. Again. It was her third time today checking up on Zoë and it was barely three o'clock. She'd been doing this all week, watching over Zoë like a mother hen. "You can stop hovering. I'm fine."

She flashed Zoë a squinty-eyed assessing look. After a few seconds, her face softened, as if she was satisfied that Zoë was being honest. "You know where I am if you need me," she said, then disappeared down the hall.

Word of what happened had traveled through the entire office in record time. She'd received several flower arrangements and sympathy cards over the weekend. They had been addressed to both her and Nick, so that cat was definitely out of the bag. Not that she cared. Everyone would have found out soon enough. They also knew that she and Nick were getting married.

Several men in his crew had wanted to throw him a bachelor party tonight, but he said that in light of what they had just been through, he didn't think it was appropriate. Zoë had said the same thing when the girls in the office had approached her about a trip across the Ambassador Bridge to the male strip club in Windsor.

She just wanted to get this wedding over and done with. Every day she waited she was more anxious, more worried that she would make it all the way to the altar only to have him say he couldn't go through with it.

Or what if he didn't show up at all? They were taking the traditional route and spending the night before their wedding apart. Nick's idea. She was staying home and he was bunking with O'Connell in his condo. Maybe she should have insisted they drive together, so she could at least be sure he would make an appearance.

She nearly groaned out loud.

This was ridiculous. She was being silly and paranoid. Of course he was going to show up. Not only was he going to show up, but he was going to marry her. Even if he hadn't actually said that he loved her.

In less than twenty-four hours she would be Mrs. Nick Bateman. Someone's *wife*. A month ago that fact would have given her hives, but for some reason the idea of getting married didn't seem all that weird to her anymore. She'd changed over the past few weeks. Being with Nick had made her realize that sharing her life with someone didn't mean sacrificing her freedom. It didn't mean compromising herself as a person.

She didn't even mind having his big dumb dog around. In fact, they felt a lot like a family. And someday their little family would grow to include children. A little boy with Nick's dimples and hazel eyes, or maybe a little girl with Zoë's curly hair and stubborn streak.

The possibilities were endless.

Tiffany from accounting barged into her office without knocking—the way she always did—and dropped an invoice on Zoë's desk.

"I need this approved," she snapped.

Nice, Zoë thought. It was common knowledge that Tiffany had been after Nick for the better part of her first six months working here. According to Shannon, Tiffany had been convinced she was next in line after the Lynn relationship had tanked, but Nick had completely blown off her very obvious advances. When she reduced herself to bluntly asking him out, he'd told her very politely—because that was his way—to give it a rest.

She was young, big-breasted and beautiful, and probably not used to men telling her no. Since she had caught Zoë and Nick playing tonsil hockey in the office that day, her panties had been in a serious twist and Zoë had been on the receiving end of a whole lotta attitude.

What Tiffany didn't seem to realize is that Zoë had the authority to fire her jealous little behind— and probably would have if the girl wasn't such a hard worker.

"I'll get this back to you by Monday," Zoë said, hoping Tiffany would take the hint and leave.

She didn't.

"So, tomorrow's the big day, huh?"

"Yup," Zoë replied, pretending to be engrossed by the open file on her computer screen. If you ignored a pest, it was supposed to go away, right?

"Considering Nick's reputation, aren't you nervous?"

Just ignore her, she told herself. She's only trying to get a rise out of you. She looked up, forcing what she hoped passed for a patient smile, but probably looked more like a grimace. "Tiffany, I'm a little busy here."

Tiffany went on as if Zoë hadn't already, in a round about way, told her to get lost. "I'm just worried about you. I'm sure you're feeling vulnerable right now."

Oh please! Now she was going to pretend to be concerned for Zoë's welfare? What an absolute crock.

"I appreciate your concern." *Not.* "But I feel a little uncomfortable discussing personal matters with you."

"You have to be at least a little worried," she persisted. "I mean, before he had a reason to marry you. And now, well…" She trailed off and let the statement hang in the air for Zoë to absorb.

And it did. Zoë had to struggle against the urge to vault over the desk and claw Tiffany's eyes out.

What Tiffany was really saying, was that Zoë was no longer pregnant, so Nick would have no reason to marry her. She couldn't deny the trickle of icy fear that slid through her veins. Because nothing Tiffany said was untrue. Bitchy and rude, yes, but not necessarily inconceivable.

"It would be bad enough being left at the altar, but what if he didn't even show up?"

Zoë's fists clenched tightly in her lap. *Don't kill her. Don't kill her,* she chanted to herself. But oh how good it would feel to blacken one of her pretty blue eyes. Or hell, maybe both of them. Tiffany may have been eight years younger and a head taller, but Zoë was pretty sure she could take her.

"Shut up, Tiffany," Shannon snapped from the doorway, appearing like an angel of mercy. "You're just jealous because you asked Nick out and he turned you down flat."

Tiffany's cheeks blushed a bright crimson and she shot Shannon a nasty look. "My money is on Nick dumping her. I guess we'll just see, won't we?"

She stomped from the room and Shannon mumbled, "What a bitch."

Zoë leaned back in her seat and exhaled deeply. "If you hadn't come in just now, I could see a possible assault charge in my very near future."

"Don't listen to her, Zoë. She has no idea what she's talking about."

"What did she mean by her money?" Zoë asked, even though she already had a pretty good idea.

"Just ignore her."

"What did she mean, Shannon?"

Shannon bit her lip, looking very uncomfortable. "I wasn't going to tell you…"

"It's another pool, isn't it?" Just what she needed, the employees betting on her getting her heart sliced and diced.

Shannon nodded, and Zoë's heart plummeted. She felt like going home, crawling into bed, covering her head and staying there forever.

"What are they betting on exactly this time?" she asked, trying to keep her voice light. Pretending that she didn't feel hurt and betrayed by people she considered her friends.

"They're betting on whether or not Nick will marry you, dump you at the altar, or not show up at all."

Zoë felt physically ill. Her voice shook when she asked, "Where did you put your money? Do you think he's going to dump me?"

"I didn't bet on this one, but if I had, I would have put my money on Nick marrying you. No question. In my life I've never known two people more perfect for each other."

"You don't think he was marrying me because of the baby?"

"As far as I'm concerned, the pregnancy just sped things up a bit. I don't doubt that he wants kids, and maybe that had been a motivating factor before when he asked those other women to marry him, but this is different. I know it is."

Zoë wanted to believe that, but she had to admit, she had doubts. Maybe if he would just tell her he loved her.

If by some miracle he didn't leave her at the altar, if they actually got married, did she want to spend her life with a man who just liked her a lot? Didn't she deserve better than that?

"It's all going to work out," Shannon assured her.

She used to think so, now she wasn't so sure. The question was, what did she plan to do about it?

"Are you sure you don't want me to be there?" Faith asked for the billionth time. "I could hop in the car and if I do ninety all the way I can be there just in time for the wedding."

Three hours, Zoë thought. She was marrying Nick in three hours. It seemed so unreal.

She'd slept in fits and bursts last night and crawled out of bed before the crack of dawn. She was too nervous to eat. Too distracted to do much more than sit at the kitchen table sipping her tea and skimming the newspaper.

According to the *Oakland Press,* the temperature would reach the midsixties with sunny skies all day. She couldn't ask for better weather.

It was her wedding day for heaven's sake! She should be happy. So why couldn't she work up a bit of enthusiasm? She hadn't even managed to drag herself into the shower yet and the dress she and Shannon had spent all day Wednesday shopping for still hung wrapped in plastic in the backseat of her car.

"Zoë?" Faith asked.

"I'm not even sure if I'm going," she admitted.

"Don't even talk like that. I've never seen you so happy. I know you've been through a lot in the past week. Maybe Nick is right, maybe you should wait a while and plan a real wedding. One your family and friends can attend."

And risk being dumped at the altar in front of the entire Simmons clan? Don't think so.

"I've just got prewedding jitters," she told her sister, so she wouldn't actually jump in the car and come down. "Everything will be great."

"Nick loves you."

"I know he does."

But therein lay the problem. She really *didn't* know. Nick hadn't said so, and she'd been too much of a chicken to come right out and ask him.

What if he said no?

Sorry, Zoë, I'm not capable of love, but I sure do like you a lot.

"I have to let you go so I can get ready," Zoë said.

"You're sure you're okay?"

"I'm fine." Lie, lie lie. She was *so* not fine.

"You'll call me later and let me know how it went?"

"I promise."

She hung up the phone and sighed, still not ready to drag herself to the bathroom for a shower. Instead she made herself another cup of tea and sat back down at the table.

Two hours later she was still sitting there, and only then did it sink in that she couldn't do it. She couldn't marry him.

The question now was, what would she tell Nick?

Thirteen

Nick stood in the lobby of the courthouse, alternating between watching the door, checking the time on his watch and pulling his phone from his pocket to make sure it was still on. His starched shirt was stiff and uncomfortable under his suit coat and his new tie was beginning to feel like a noose around his neck.

He'd tried Zoë's house phone and cell but she hadn't answered. He'd even called Faith, then spoke to Shannon in the office, but no one had heard from her for hours.

A smart man, a *realistic* man, would have left a long time ago. Right after he realized his fiancée was, in fact, not going to show up for their wedding.

He should have been at least a little angry at Zoë

for leaving him high and dry, but the truth was, he had it coming.

He deserved this.

In fact, he was glad she'd done it. It was the push he'd needed to realize just how much of an ass he'd been.

What reason had he given Zoë for believing he would marry her? Hell, as far as she knew, he might not have even shown up. Sure he'd said he wanted to marry her, but he'd fed the same line to two other women.

What he had failed to do was prove to Zoë that she was different. That she was the *one*.

He loved her, and he should have told her so.

And it's not as if he hadn't had chances. That night when they had made love and she had told him she loved him, he could have said he loved her, too. And later, when he'd admitted to her that he'd never said the words. He could have told her then.

He could have said it in the hospital, or any time the entire next day they had spent side-by-side, mourning their loss. So many times the words had been balanced on the tip of his tongue, ready to be spoken, but something always stopped him. He had always held back.

Maybe that was simply what he had taught himself to do. His mother had been the only one who loved him and she'd left. By no fault of her own, but that hadn't made it hurt any less.

His aunt and uncle might have loved him, but if they had, they never said so. As he grew up, it was just easier not letting anyone get too close. Not letting himself fall in love.

Talk about a cliché. But clichés were born for a reason, weren't they? Maybe deep down he was still that little boy who was afraid to get his heart broken again.

But it was too late, he was in love with Zoë. The only thing he'd accomplished by keeping that to himself was hurting her.

"I love her," he said to himself, surprised to find that it wasn't that hard to say at all. In fact, he liked the sound of it, the feel of the words forming in his mouth.

It felt…natural.

He pushed off the wall and headed for the stairs, knowing exactly what he needed to do.

It was time he said goodbye to the little boy and started acting like a man.

Zoë wasn't sure how long after their scheduled wedding Nick finally showed up. She sat alone on the swing in the backyard, still in her pajamas, with her legs pulled up and her knees tucked under her chin, wondering if he actually *would* show up. Maybe he was so angry he would never speak to her again.

But then the backdoor had opened and Nick walked through, still dressed in his suit. He crossed the lawn to the swing, hands tucked in the pockets of his slacks, looking more tired than angry.

And boy did he look good in a suit. Almost as good as he looked out of it.

What was wrong with her? She just stood the guy up and now she's picturing him naked?

"You seem to have forgotten that we had a date this afternoon."

She cringed and looked up at him apologetically. "I am so sorry, Nick."

"No." He sat beside her on the swing, loosening his tie. "I'm the one who's sorry."

He didn't hate her after all, not that she ever really believed he would. Maybe she thought she deserved it. "This is completely my fault. I guess I just…got scared."

"Scared that I would back out at the last minute. Or possibly not show up at all?"

She nodded, thankful that he said it for her. And even more thankful that he understood.

"I gave you no reason to believe otherwise." He took her hand and held it, lacing his fingers through hers. "Which makes this entire mess very much my fault."

"I should have trusted you."

He laughed, but there wasn't a trace of humor in the sound. "What did I ever do to earn your trust? Ask you to marry me? Stick a ring on your finger? Well, so what? I did the same thing with two other women and I'm not married to either of them, am I?"

Jeez, twist the knife a little deeper why don't you? Was he *trying* to make her feel worse?

"Um, I'm not quite sure what your point is, but for the record, this isn't helping."

"My point is, I knew exactly what you needed

from me, but I was too much of a coward to give it to you. That line I fed you about the ring making it official was bull. The only way to make this relationship official is for me to stop acting like an ass and tell you how I feel."

"I could have asked," she said.

He shot her a look. "You shouldn't have to."

No, she shouldn't, which is probably why she hadn't. Call her stubborn and a little old-fashioned, but she believed that when you felt a certain way about someone, you told them so.

He cupped her chin in his hand and lifted her face to his. "I never thought it was possible to love someone as much as I love you. Maybe that's why I didn't let myself trust it."

She could feel tears welling in her eyes and burning her nose, and she didn't even have those pesky hormones as an excuse this time.

He kissed her gently. "I love you, Zoë. With all my heart."

She closed her eyes and sighed. No words had ever sounded sweeter or meant so much. Because she knew they came directly from his heart. "I love you too, Nick."

"I have a favor to ask. This is going to sound a little strange, but I'm asking you to trust me."

"Okay."

"Could I possibly have that ring back for a minute?"

It was a little strange, but she trusted him. She slipped it off her finger and set it in his hand.

"I figured it was about time I do this right." He slid off the swing and got down on one knee in front of her. Zoë held her breath and the tears that had been hovering inside her lids began to spill over. "Zoë Simmons, would you do me the honor of becoming my wife?"

"Absolutely," she said. He slipped the ring back on her finger and she threw her arms around his neck and hugged him.

"I know you didn't want a big wedding, but I don't think you have much choice now."

She pulled back and looked at him. He had a very sly, devious grin on that gorgeous face. "Why?"

"Because when I hung up the phone after asking your parents' permission to marry you, they were already working on the guest list."

Her mouth fell open. "You called and asked their *permission?*"

He grinned. "I told you, I wanted to do it right this time."

Oh my gosh, she was now officially daughter of the year. And only a couple of weeks ago she'd been worried about excommunication. "So what did you say?"

"I told them I was in love with you, and I wanted their permission to marry you."

She couldn't believe he'd actually asked permission. "What did they say?"

He grinned. "They both said, it's about time."

Epilogue

Nick trudged down the stairs to the first floor, side-stepping to avoid the half-naked Barbie doll lying in the hallway and kicking aside a handful of Matchbox cars in the den doorway. This all should have been picked up by now.

When he saw the video game on the television screen, he knew why it wasn't.

He crossed the room and shut the television off and received a collective, *"Daaaaaaad!"* from their oldest children, nine-year-old Steven and eight-year-old Lila.

"Don't dad me. You're supposed to be cleaning up your toys. It's almost bedtime."

Six-year-old Nathan, who had inherited not only his father's dark hair and hazel eyes, but also his clean gene, was already working diligently to get all the LEGOS put back in their bin.

"Jenny burped," he said, pointing to the six-month-old tucked under Nick's left arm. The one struggling and squirming to get down and practice the new crawling thing she'd mastered just yesterday.

He didn't have a burp cloth handy, so he wiped away the spit-up with the hem of his shirt, wondering if a day had passed in the last nine years when he hadn't walked around with the remains of someone else's dinner on his clothes.

"Daddy!" four-year-old Olivia, the outspoken one of the bunch, screeched from the doorway, not three feet away. She had two volumes. Loud, and *really* loud. "Mommy is in the kitchen eating cookies again."

He crouched down in front of her, and being closer to the floor and freedom, Jenny let out an earsplitting squeal and struggled to get loose. "Liv' honey, what did Mommy and Daddy tell you about tattling?"

Olivia's lower lip curled into her signature pout. "I want cookies, too."

"Not before bed."

"Then why does Mommy get to eat cookies before bed?" Nathan asked.

"Because she's a grown-up," Lila said, giving him a shove as she walked past him. "She can eat cookies whenever she wants."

"You can have cookies tomorrow," Nick told her.

"She ate like the whole box," Steven mumbled. "There won't be any left tomorrow."

"Hey, mister, I heard that." Zoë stood in the den doorway, hands on her hips. Her hair hung in damp tendrils from a recent bath and her pink robe was conspicuously dotted with cookie crumbs. "Lila, can you please watch your sister for a minute? Daddy and I need to have a quick meeting."

"Sure, Mom!" she said, brightly, taking her baby sister from Nick's arms. Watching Jenny meant she didn't have to clean.

Zoë motioned him out of the room, mumbling, "Five kids. Whose bright idea was that?"

It hadn't actually been anyone's *idea*. After Steven and Lila, who were both carefully planned, they figured they had their boy and girl, so they were all set. But then Lila had started getting a little bit older and Zoë started having those baby cravings again.

They were a little lax with the contraceptives thinking that if it was meant to be, it was meant to be, and along came Nathan nine months later. Olivia was their first real oops baby, and the result of a bit too much champagne on New Year's Eve.

Jenny, oops baby number two, had been conceived when they thought they were being careful. Obviously not careful enough, her doctor had said when the test came back positive.

After Jenny was born, to avoid any further oopses, her doctor had finally put her on the pill. It was wreaking havoc on her menstrual cycle, and she'd been awfully weepy lately, but thank God it appeared to be working. Their only other option had been a vasectomy. Either that or he would have to move into an apartment down the street since after almost eleven years of marriage he still couldn't seem to keep his hands off her.

She led him to the first floor meeting room—the half bath next to the kitchen. One of the few places besides their bedroom that they could truly be alone.

She turned to him, her cheeks rosy from her bath, her eyes bright. It amazed him sometimes how much he loved her. It was as if, once he opened up his heart to her, it went a little crazy making up for lost time.

Each time he thought he couldn't possibly love her more than he already did, he would hear her reading Olivia a bedtime story, changing her voice for all the different characters, or he would catch her blowing raspberries on Jenny's belly while she changed her diaper. There were a million little things she did that made him love her more every day.

He might have been worried that he loved her too much, but she felt the exact same way about him.

"What's up?" he asked.

She blew out a big breath and said, "We have a problem."

He frowned. "What kind of problem?"

"Well, not a problem exactly, more like a slight inconvenience."

He folded his arms across his chest and sighed. "What did they break this time?"

"Nothing was broken. You know how my periods have been screwy since Jenny was born."

"Yeah?"

She bit her lip. "And, um, how I've been feeling a little yucky lately? Really tired and kinda nauseous."

Uh-oh, he had a feeling he knew where this was going. "I thought that was from the birth control."

"So did I. At first."

"But?"

"But then I noticed that it had been a while since I had my period."

"So what you're saying is, you're late."

She nodded. "I'm late."

He took a big breath and blew it out. Here we go again. "How late?"

"Two weeks, maybe three."

He raised an eyebrow at her. "Which is it, two or three?"

She bit her lip again. "Um, probably closer to three."

"Does this mean I need to make a trip to the pharmacy and get a test?"

"I went four days ago before I picked the kids up from school."

"*Four* days?"

She shrugged. "Denial. I finally worked up the courage to take it tonight after my bath."

Asking was merely a formality at this point. "And?"

She sighed. "Oops."

He tried not to smile, but he could feel a grin tugging at the corners of his mouth.

She rolled her eyes. "I know you're happy about this so you might as well just go ahead and smile."

He gripped the lapels of her robe and tugged her to him, brushing a kiss across her lips. "I love you."

"Six kids," she said, shaking her head. She looked a little shell-shocked, but he could tell she was happy, too.

The truth was, they could have six more and she wouldn't hear a complaint from him. He had plenty of love in his heart to go around.

"Not bad for a woman who once said she never wanted kids."

"Steven will be barely ten when the baby's born meaning we will have six kids under the age of eleven." She ran her fingers through the hair at his temples that had just begun to turn gray. "We must be completely nuts."

"Probably," he agreed, but insanity was highly underrated.

"I guess this is what I get for marrying a man who wanted a big family, huh?"

"Yeah, because you know what they say."

She thought about it for a second then said, "Fools rush in where angels fear to tread?"

He grinned. "Be careful what you wish for, you just might get it."

* * * * *

Happily ever after is just the beginning...

Turn the page for a sneak preview of
DANCING ON SUNDAY AFTERNOONS
by
Linda Cardillo

Harlequin Everlasting—Every great love
has a story to tell. ™
A brand-new line from Harlequin Books
launching this February!

Prologue

Giulia D'Orazio
1983

I had two husbands—Paolo and Salvatore.

Salvatore and I were married for thirty-two years. I still live in the house he bought for us; I still sleep in our bed. All around me are the signs of our life together. My bedroom window looks out over the garden he planted. In the middle of the city, he coaxed tomatoes, peppers, zucchini—even grapes for his wine—out of the ground. On weekends, he used to drive up to his cousin's farm in Waterbury and bring back manure. In the winter, he wrapped the peach tree and the fig tree with rags and black rubber hoses against the cold, his massive, coarse hands gentling those trees as if they were his fragile-skinned babies. My neighbor, Dominic Grazza, does that for me now. My boys have no time for the garden.

In the front of the house, Salvatore planted roses. The roses I take care of myself. They are giant, cream-colored, fragrant. In the afternoons, I like to sit out on the porch with my coffee, protected from the eyes of the neighborhood by that curtain of flowers.

Salvatore died in this house thirty-five years ago. In the last months, he lay on the sofa in the parlor so he could be in the middle of everything. Except for the two oldest boys, all the children were still at home and we ate together every evening. Salvatore could see the dining room table from the sofa, and he could hear everything that was said. "I'm not dead, yet," he told me. "I want to know what's going on."

When my first grandchild, Cara, was born, we brought her to him, and he held her on his chest, stroking her tiny head. Sometimes they fell asleep together.

Over on the radiator cover in the corner of the parlor is the portrait Salvatore and I had taken on our twenty-fifth anniversary. This brooch I'm wearing today, with the diamonds—I'm wearing it in the photograph also—Salvatore gave it to me that day. Upstairs on my dresser is a jewelry box filled with necklaces and bracelets and earrings. All from Salvatore.

I am surrounded by the things Salvatore gave me,

or did for me. But, God forgive me, as I lie alone now in my bed, it is Paolo I remember.

Paolo left me nothing. Nothing, that is, that my family, especially my sisters, thought had any value. No house. No diamonds. Not even a photograph.

But after he was gone, and I could catch my breath from the pain, I knew that I still had something. In the middle of the night, I sat alone and held them in my hands, reading the words over and over until I heard his voice in my head. I had Paolo's letters.

* * * * *

Be sure to look for
DANCING ON SUNDAY AFTERNOONS
available January 30, 2007.
And look, too, for our other
Everlasting title available,

FALL FROM GRACE by Kristi Gold.

FALL FROM GRACE is a deeply emotional story
of what a long-term love really means.
As Jack and Anne Morgan discover,
marriage vows can be broken—but
they can be mended, too.
And the memories of their marriage
have an unexpected power to bring back
a love that never really left....

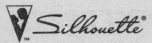

REQUEST YOUR FREE BOOKS!

2 FREE NOVELS
PLUS 2
FREE GIFTS!

Silhouette®

Desire®

Passionate, Powerful, Provocative!

YES! Please send me 2 FREE Silhouette Desire® novels and my 2 FREE gifts. After receiving them, if I don't wish to receive any more books, I can return the shipping statement marked "cancel." If I don't cancel, I will receive 6 brand-new novels every month and be billed just $3.80 per book in the U.S., or $4.47 per book in Canada, plus 25¢ shipping and handling per book and applicable taxes, if any*. That's a savings of almost 15% off the cover price! I understand that accepting the 2 free books and gifts places me under no obligation to buy anything. I can always return a shipment and cancel at any time. Even if I never buy another book from Silhouette, the two free books and gifts are mine to keep forever.

225 SDN EEXJ 326 SDN EEXU

Name	(PLEASE PRINT)	
Address		Apt.
City	State/Prov.	Zip/Postal Code

Signature (if under 18, a parent or guardian must sign)

Mail to Silhouette Reader Service™:

IN U.S.A.	**IN CANADA**
P.O. Box 1007	P.O. Box 609
Buffalo, NY	Fort Erie, Ontario
14240-1867	L2A 5X3

Not valid to current Silhouette Desire subscribers.

Want to try two free books from another line?
Call 1-800-873-8635 or visit www.morefreebooks.com.

* Terms and prices subject to change without notice. NY residents add applicable sales tax. Canadian residents will be charged applicable provincial taxes and GST. This offer is limited to one order per household. All orders subject to approval. Credit or debit balances in a customer's account(s) may be offset by any other outstanding balance owed by or to the customer. Please allow 4 to 6 weeks for delivery.

SDES06

HARLEQUIN
Super Romance®

Is it really possible to find true love
when you're single...with kids?

Introducing an exciting new five-book miniseries,

SINGLES...WITH KIDS

When Margo almost loses her bistro...and custody of
her children...she realizes a real family is about more
than owning a pretty house and being a perfect mother.
And then there's the new man in her life, Robert...
Like the other single parents in her support group, she
has to make sure he wants the whole package.

Starting in February 2007 with

LOVE AND THE SINGLE MOM
by C.J. Carmichael

(Harlequin Superromance #1398)

ALSO WATCH FOR:

THE SISTER SWITCH Pamela Ford (#1404, on sale March 2007)
ALL-AMERICAN FATHER Anna DeStefano (#1410, on sale April 2007)
THE BEST-KEPT SECRET Melinda Curtis (#1416, on sale May 2007)
BLAME IT ON THE DOG Amy Frazier (#1422, on sale June 2007)

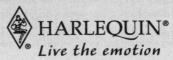

HARLEQUIN®
Live the emotion

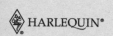

HARLEQUIN®

EVERLASTING LOVE™

Every great love has a story to tell™

Save $1.⁰⁰ off

the purchase of
any Harlequin
Everlasting Love novel

Coupon valid from January 1, 2007
until April 30, 2007.

Valid at retail outlets in the U.S. only.
Limit one coupon per customer.

5 65373 00076 2   (8100) 0 11302

HEUSCPN0107

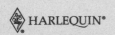

EVERLASTING LOVE™

Every great love has a story to tell™

Fall from Grace

Kristi Gold

Save $1.⁰⁰ off

the purchase of
any Harlequin
Everlasting Love novel

Coupon valid from January 1, 2007
until April 30, 2007.

**Valid at retail outlets in Canada only.
Limit one coupon per customer.**

52607370

HECDNCPN0407

HARLEQUIN® *Romance*®

What a month!

In February watch for

Rancher and Protector
Part of the Western Weddings miniseries
BY JUDY CHRISTENBERRY

The Boss's Pregnancy Proposal
BY RAYE MORGAN

Also in February, expect
MORE of what you love
as the Harlequin Romance line
increases to six titles per month.

Don't miss the first book
in THE ROYALS trilogy:

THE FORBIDDEN PRINCESS
(SD #1780)

by national bestselling author

DAY LECLAIRE

Moments before her loveless royal wedding,
Princess Alyssa was kidnapped by a mysterious man
who'd do anything to stop the ceremony. Even if that
meant marrying the forbidden princess himself!

On sale February 2007 from Silhouette Desire!

THE ROYALS
Stories of scandals and secrets
amidst the most powerful palaces.

Make sure to read the other titles in the series:
THE PRINCE'S MISTRESS
On sale March 2007
THE ROYAL WEDDING NIGHT
On sale April 2007

*Available wherever books are sold, including most
bookstores, supermarkets, discount stores and drugstores.*